"Don't risk your life just because you're still in immediate danger," Boone said.

"You're wrong," Angie said, her eyes flashing furiously.

"I am?"

"You've been wrong before."

Boone knew she was right. He considered apologizing, for thinking the evidence had disappeared because of her negligence. But he'd played the murder case the way he needed to in order to free an innocent man. He couldn't apologize for that.

"That doesn't mean I'm wrong now. Making faulty assumptions could get you killed. How about if I keep my opinions to myself and tag along with you anyway?" he asked.

She frowned. "Why would you want to?"

Boone considered his answer carefully. Because he owed her. Because he thought she was wrong about the threat to her life and didn't want her to be dead wrong. Because...

"Because I missed you."

FLORENCE CASE's

favorite novels in her preteen years were the Dana Girls and Nancy Drew series about teenage sleuths solving mysteries, and Grace Livingston Hill's inspirational romances. Her first work of fiction was in fifth grade — a two-page mystery, which the teacher loved. She kept writing during her teenage years, earning her B.A. in German, marrying her wonderful husband and moving from New Jersey to the Deep South. The birth of her beloved son with his mental handicaps and autism, and all the struggles of raising him, drew her closer to God, and she felt called to write for the Lord. In addition to writing, she teaches the adult Sunday School class in her church and works the soundboard for the singing group her son belongs to, which visits nursing homes. You can contact Florence through www.shoutlife.com/FlorenceCase.

DEADLY Reunion

FLORENCE CASE

Steeple Hill®

Published by Steeple Hill Books™

STEEPLE HILL BOOKS

Steeple Hill®

Recycling programs for this product may not exist in your area.

ISBN-13: 978-0-373-44328-4
ISBN-10:   0-373-44328-5

DEADLY REUNION

Copyright © 2009 by Florence Moyer

www.SteepleHill.com

Printed in U.S.A.

Be kind to one another, tenderhearted,
forgiving each other, just as God in Christ
also has forgiven you.
—*Ephesians* 4:32

Thank you to my support ladies: Misty, Barrie, Kathy, Alli, Danita and Maureen, who hung in there with me.

Above all, a special thank you to my editor, Melissa Endlich. I am still in the clouds.

ONE

Seeing the dead body of her friend and mentor two days ago had been bad enough—seeing her ex-fiancé's alive and breathing one in less than a minute was going to be torture. But Angie Delitano had examined the situation she suddenly found herself in from every angle, and out of all the people she couldn't trust right now, Boone Walker was the only one she was certain was not involved. So here she was, going to a man who had betrayed her for help.

How dumb was that?

Resting her hand on the knob that would open the door to the Walker law firm, she took a deep breath. What to say? How to act? Six months ago, after he'd shredded her reputation—and her heart—she'd left Boone's engagement ring on the witness stand in front of a packed courtroom, vowing never to lay eyes on him again. But earlier today, she'd found out she no longer had the luxury of that choice.

Someone had threatened her life.

So now her insides were doing jumping jacks, and her emotions were on the verge of boiling over. Having to go to Boone for help made her want to hit something. He'd been willing to wreck her reputation to defend a suspected wife-murderer, forgetting all about how he supposedly *loved* her. Worse, Boone's expert defense of the man—who she still believed with all her instincts and heart *had* murdered his wife—had freed the creep…who was now dating her sister.

"Cope," she ordered herself. She willed the tears burning behind her eyes to go away. Luckily she was a cop and had plenty of practice in appearing cool and detached, even when her heart was breaking for a victim. She would need that facade in front of Boone. She couldn't let him think she might actually still care about him.

Because there was no way she could, right?

Resolutely, Angie turned the knob and opened the door, once again the in-control, never-say-die police officer. Her sister's life—and maybe her own—depended on her getting Boone as a backup this morning. After that, she could really walk away and pretend he didn't exist.

Which suited her just fine.

What on earth…? Boone Walker watched his former fiancée launch herself into his office for the first time in months. Thanks to years in the courtroom, where the unexpected often happened, he was able to sit back calmly and pin his well-cultivated, steady stare on her, concealing the confusion her sudden appearance caused inside him. After she'd left his ring on the witness stand, Angie hadn't answered his phone calls or shown any signs of wanting to talk things over—so why now? It didn't make sense.

Unless…something was terribly wrong and she was desperate. Or maybe…she was finally ready to talk?

His new secretary, Karen, appeared right behind Angie with an apologetic look. "I'm sorry. I asked her to let me announce her, but she said there was no need, you knew who she was."

"Don't worry about it. Tornadoes are hard to stop," Boone said. His secretary sent him a faint smile, but Angie kept her cool, "can't touch me" look.

Waving Karen out, he waited until she closed the door, then turned his attention to the woman he'd almost married. He thought of a hundred things to say. "Are you okay?" "Am I under arrest?" "Funny seeing you here." But he lost his mind and instead said, "I missed you."

For only a few seconds, her pine-green eyes, shaded by thick black lashes, softened. She splayed her fingertips through her chin-length, pale blond waves, a sure sign she was flustered; Boone watched her in fascination, like he'd always done. He doubted she realized how much she'd captivated him from the moment he'd first seen her well over a year ago. Or how much it bothered him to do what he'd had to in court months later.

The uncertainty in her eyes was either that she didn't believe he'd missed her at all, or that she was second-guessing herself for coming here. It couldn't be the last part—Angie Delitano hadn't had an indecisive moment in all the time he'd known her. Not even in the courtroom that day. She'd left his ring behind and, just like his mom where his dad was concerned, never looked back.

He needed to remember that.

"Talk to me, Angie."

"Things have happened this week," she said. "Bad things."

"I heard about Cliff Haggis's suicide." Boone never would have guessed the seasoned detective, Angie's mentor at the station, capable of suicide. But neither was he surprised. Being a cop was hard anywhere, and Copper City, even though it was a lot smaller than nearby Cincinnati and had a lower-than-average crime rate, was no exception.

"I'm sorry," he added, tapping the pile of papers at the side of his desk to distract himself. Relating to people on an emotional level was not easy for him, but even he knew how to be polite. "I know he was a good friend of yours."

"Yeah, he was," she said. She took a long breath, and he

watched her slim fingers alternately grip and let loose of the oversize, chocolate leather handbag she had in her arms.

"Sit?" he invited with a gesture of his hand toward his client chair, since she seemed about to run away. She folded her slim, graceful build onto the seat, her face once again wearing what he thought of as her "cop stare." She'd used it for the first time when he was ripping apart her testimony. He had a feeling before this day was through, he'd see the stare over and over again.

The detached look probably meant she wasn't there to talk about their ruined relationship, or to set it right. That was fine by him. She'd hurt him badly when she'd been unwilling to understand his absolute need to do what he'd done and then broken their engagement—but he'd forced himself to recover. He refused to be his father, pining after a woman who couldn't understand why he was the way he was.

"Indirectly," Angie said, glancing at his once again tapping fingers, "my being here has to do with Cliff's death. He told me something before he died, and I was on my way to investigate what he said this morning, but then something happened, and I don't know if I can trust anyone at the precinct now." She took a breath and gazed into his eyes. "All I am certain of is that I can trust you with my life."

The air went out of Boone as her words about believing in him dug into his heart. He stilled his fingers.

"So I decided to put our past aside temporarily," she added. "While I can't say I'm happy about what you did to my reputation in court, I have to admit you tried to warn me ahead of time about your loyalty to your clients. They come first."

Angie was correct, and that brought Boone no joy whatsoever. He *had* indirectly hurt her so he could get an innocent man freed. And he was sorry he'd had to. But he couldn't be any different than he was, and that meant she was better off without him. And he was better off without a woman who was going to get in the way of his mission.

"But your loyalty to them also showed me," Angie continued, "that if you give me your word you will help me, just like you help your clients, you'll be there for me."

Boone continued to stare at her. His first inclination—and heartfelt desire—was to say "of course, whatever you need, just ask," but he couldn't voice the words. He had rebuilt the emotional wall around himself that she'd broken through when they met and fell in love, and was refocused on his passion for helping people who had been falsely accused of crimes, like his father had been. He was, if not happy, at least content. Being around her again, even for a little while, could change all that. Divert him from his true purpose. He didn't think it was worth chancing.

On the other side of the argument, Boone knew how alone Angie was. He couldn't stand it when people had no one to turn to. Especially women. Besides, he owed her…something.

"Never mind," she said, rising and swiping her indigo jeans with her hand as though she were brushing him off. "This was a mistake, coming here. I don't know what I was thinking." Pivoting, she headed across the thick emerald carpeting to the door, making no sound.

Her every step farther away from him squeezed Boone's heart painfully. Man, he was no good at stuff like this. He needed to let her go.

Let her go.

"You haven't even said what kind of help you need, Angie."

She turned and stared at him again, working her shiny pink bottom lip back and forth slowly. "There was a time," she said slowly, "you wouldn't have needed to ask. You would have just agreed to help me."

Boone tore his gaze from her lips to her eyes. He could see

the deep pain she felt from having to come to him for help, and for a few seconds, he longed to wipe away that pain. To fix everything between them. But that was impossible. They were just too different.

"I'm treating you like a client, remember? Your rules."

"I'm going to regret this," she said with a doomsday sense of drama. "I know I'm going to regret this."

Him, too. "Give me a try anyway."

She remained on the other side of his office. Boone welcomed the distance from the woman so he could pay more attention to what she would say instead of how lovely her eyes were. At least it ought to have worked that way. From this perspective, though, he was only reminded of how willowy her frame was, and how gracefully she moved. And how much he missed her presence in his life.

Strange how getting hurt didn't dissolve attraction.

"As I said, before Cliff…died…he gave me some information. A message on my answering machine. That missing murder weapon in the Detry case?"

The weapon he'd let the jury think Angie had either not really seen or had lost track of? The missing evidence that had brought about the end of their engagement and his dreams for the wonderful family he'd always wanted? Yeah, he knew that weapon. Tensing, not wanting to fight with her over a trial that could not be changed, he nodded.

"Cliff said that he took the evidence and buried it, and then let me take the heat for it."

"That doesn't make sense." Cliff Haggis and his wife had taken Angie under their wing when Angie's former husband, a no-good drug dealer, had been killed in a shootout with the police. They'd also led her to a relationship with Christ, one that Boone didn't understand and felt no hope of ever achieving. "Cliff was one of the good guys."

"Yeah. Rude awakening, huh? Most of the rest of his message was basically an apology for helping to wreck my life."

Boone had read in the paper how Angie was investigated by her department for negligence—because of his innuendoes in the Detry trial—and that the investigation had been dropped for lack of conclusive evidence one way or another.

"Most of the rest?" Boone asked. "What else did he say?"

"That he was trying to make things right. He told me to dig up the gun, clear my reputation, but then to let the dead rest in peace. That doing anything else was too dangerous. I was worried about him and wanted more of an explanation than he was giving, so I went over there. The front door was open, and he was on the couch."

She took a shaky breath. "Suicide is what they're saying. But I have no idea why he would do that." She paused and gazed at him. "It was brutal."

Boone saw the shock at the discovery still in her eyes, heard her voice falter, but once again, he wasn't sure what to say beyond platitudes. Words never failed him while arguing a case, but the second emotions came into play, his vocabulary dried up. He'd discovered that after he and Angie got engaged and the first problem between them arose. He'd never figured out how to help her feel better—he wished he had. Maybe things would have been...

Don't go there, he warned himself.

For over a minute, they just looked at each other. Angie shook off the pain over Cliff and drank in the sight of Boone's broad shoulders, squared-off jaw and penetrating, royal-blue eyes as if he were lifesaving water. That was okay—as long as she remembered that too much of that water could drown her.

Exhaling a quick breath from her mouth, she returned to the front of his desk, where she again plopped down in the client chair, almost as opulent as his own, and let her bag fall onto the carpet in a chocolate heap. Boone remained in his seat behind the mahogany monstrosity he called a desk.

She'd blinked first because it was hard to look at the man and not want him to take her in his arms—especially from the instant Boone had said he missed her and traded his distant look for a concerned one. Concerned was good. Good as long as she kept her head over it, got his help and then left him behind.

Because in reality, his concern meant nothing. He'd shown the same emotion for Warren Detry, the wife-murderer she'd arrested who Boone had sworn was innocent. Concern wasn't love. Not even Boone's interest in her from the moment they'd met, she'd come to realize, was love. She wasn't going to fool herself again—she just wasn't someone anyone could love. Hadn't her own mother shown her that?

But she was getting lost in the past, and Boone was waiting for her to continue.

She swallowed down a lump in her throat. *Cope.* "Trouble is, Cliff wasn't exactly clear about where the evidence was, and I wasn't able to ask him." She arced her hands in the air in frustration. "I could only figure he meant some of the message as a puzzle, trying to make sure he didn't leave behind any information that might get into the wrong hands. He loved word puzzles. It took me a while, but I came up with one idea about the references to digging up evidence long buried and letting the dead rest in peace. It might mean he buried the gun at Detry's wife's gravesite."

"You think?"

"I don't know. There's too much about this whole thing I don't understand. Why he had to kill himself…" She shook her head slowly. "I especially don't get that. But there's more."

"I kind of figured, or you would've brought the weapon here gift wrapped with an 'I told you so.'"

Her smile was spontaneous. She could have shot herself for not holding it back, for as soon as Boone saw her grin, his solemn blue eyes took on that twinkle she remembered all too well. *Peachy.*

"I like making you smile," he told her.

"Well, don't like it too much."

Instead of being irritated, he just grinned. She pretended not to melt a little, but it was hard. *Diversion needed.*

"This is where the 'something happened' part comes in," she continued. "Before I came here, I was headed to the Last Stop Cemetery, where Laurie Detry is buried, and I stopped for coffee. When I came out to my car, I found a nasty little death threat under my windshield wiper. It warned me to forget what I think I know about the murder or I'm dead."

Boone muttered a curse and his face darkened, surprising Angie. She'd never seen him look this angry. Sure, he had a heart for the underdog, and in this particular situation, she was the one barking. But he always hid his emotions from clients. Surely he didn't see her as anything more than that? He understood it was over between them, didn't he?

Not wanting to get into that—ever—she regrouped. "I could try to handle finding the evidence on my own, but if the missing evidence is buried there, I thought it might be smart to have someone watch my back while I'm busy digging."

"Really smart," Boone agreed.

"So will you help?"

"Of course."

His instant response was a good sign. She was happy he was so willing to play bodyguard, but niggling little doubts immediately started to chomp away at that happiness. What if he really did have the wrong idea about a future for them?

"No strings attached," she warned.

"Wasn't even thinking in that direction," Boone replied easily.

Too easily. Angie's eyes narrowed. "Neither was I." Really. "I only came to you because it's possible someone at the department might have helped Cliff hide the weapon, and covered up for him. I don't know that anyone did, but I can't take the chance. If I hand in the evidence there, it might disappear again."

"That seems possible," he agreed. "I know the county sheriff's chief deputy personally. Once we find it, we can bring the evidence to him."

That would work. Angie nodded slowly. "I am sorry if I'm taking you away from important work—"

"Angie." Boone held up his palm. "Please, don't be nervous where I'm concerned. I can take the time for you. And I understand where things stand between us and am not reading anything into your asking me for backup."

Good. Because she was over him—over men and the idea of a husband bringing her any kind of peace and security at all. Boone had been strike two. From where she stood, she now expected that if God wanted her to be married, He'd find her a husband, and she would have no doubts about the rightness of His choice. Boone could absolutely, positively, not be the right man, because she had a whole boatload of doubts about him.

Even if he was staring at her with eyes she could dive into.

"You do realize," Boone said suddenly, "that you should get a search warrant to dig on private property?"

"The judge isn't going to give me one on total speculation, which is all my theory is. Besides, I had my fill of looking like a fool at the trial, thank you."

His eyes took on an apologetic look, which she ignored. The possibility a judge might laugh at her theory left her cold inside, and she had Boone to thank for robbing her of not only her reputation, but also her confidence in her ability as a cop. As a Christian, she had tried several times during the last half year to make the leap into forgiveness, but she couldn't, not when Boone wasn't the least bit sorry. Too much hurt lingered. And fear that if she stuck around Boone for too long, he could betray her all over again.

"You've got something else planned?" he asked.

"Instead of a warrant, I'm stopping in at the cemetery caretaker's office, telling him important evidence might be buried there, and asking for permission to search." Begging for permission, if need be.

"That should work, too." Boone nodded. "Since you don't want to go to a judge, I take it you don't want my friend from the sheriff's department coming as a witness, either, just in case the gun isn't buried there?"

"You're finally understanding me," she told him.

"Only six months too late," he said. The thought lingered in the air between them as Boone reached for a set of keys on the glass-topped surface near his phone, unlocked a desk drawer, and pulled out a Glock she knew he kept within arm's reach on purpose. He had a wide reputation for being the best criminal-defense attorney in the county, and sometimes, he'd once told her, desperate people who *were* guilty came to ask him for help. He never knew how well they would take his refusal to defend them. He'd only drawn it twice, but he would shoot if he had to.

She believed him. He always told her the truth, like when he'd said he'd do anything to keep his client from prison. She just hadn't thought that "anything" would include ruining her.

She swallowed. She had to stop the self-pity and focus. There was a life riding on it.

She watched Boone stand, pull open his black, designer suit jacket and place his weapon in a leather shoulder holster. Broad-shouldered and tall, he had a way of making her feel safe when in his presence, even when he wasn't carrying.

Not that she was worried or anything. But if she got shot from behind, who would see justice done? Leaning over, she patted her own backup weapon, a Beretta, that was lodged in an ankle holster under her jeans. "Will I be keeping you from any appointments or court appearances?"

"Not unless we get murdered."

She couldn't resist rolling her eyes at him. "Like you would let the opposition get the best of you with a little old gun. You'd probably debate him to death first."

He chuckled, but when he rounded his desk and joined her, his dark blue eyes were serious again. Angie didn't like that look on him—it meant trouble for her.

"You realize if we find this evidence, it will more than likely be inadmissible in any court, right? The chain of custody can't be proved. And since Detry's wife owned the gun to begin with, Detry's prints showing up on it won't be a shocker, unless there are blood smears with his prints on them. The only usefulness it'll have is if someone else's prints are on the grip."

"I actually hadn't thought beyond that dumping it on your desk and the 'I told you so' you mentioned earlier," Angie told him, standing. "But let's leave it up to a judge to decide if *Detry's* prints are usable." She stressed his name to make sure Boone knew she didn't doubt the outcome, even if he did. "I know he can't be retried because of double jeopardy, but maybe they can get him for perjury."

"Detry didn't lie."

What was with this one-upmanship thing? Had they always done it, but she'd been too in love with him to notice? Angie guessed it didn't matter. She was getting what she wanted, so she flattened her lips together and refused to push his buttons further.

Boone, however, wasn't as polite. "Your friend's hiding crucial evidence and lying about its existence needs to be investigated."

"If you're suggesting Cliff would murder a woman in cold blood and then hide the weapon, stop. He wouldn't. *Wouldn't have,*" she corrected, glaring at Boone. A word formed on his lips, but she interrupted him with a wave of her hand. "If you say one more word in that direction, I think I'll leave alone and risk getting shot."

"Wouldn't want that to happen. You ready?"

He'd caved in awfully fast. Angie frowned as she grabbed her handbag and walked out of the office ahead of him. He was making an effort to be helpful—she had to give him that much—but she knew better than to let her guard down around him. At least she wouldn't have to see him again past today—if all went well, that was. She didn't want to think about the alternatives. Sometimes, like when she was around Boone, it was better not to think too much.

Five minutes later they had retrieved a shovel for digging and a metal detector—both brand-spanking-new from Wal-Mart—from her trunk and got into Boone's charcoal-gray sedan with tinted windows so dark she was sure they were illegal.

"I always thought this car had a sinister aura," she said, pulling her seat belt around her. Sinister or not, she had to admit the inside smelled good. Like real leather and citrus. Then she realized the lime scent came from Boone, and butterflies fluttered in her stomach.

"I realize it's low profile for you." He turned the key, and the powerful motor came to life. "What exactly is that shade of orange you drive around in?"

"It's called *candy orange,* and it's not that bright."

"Okay, vivid."

"At least if anyone runs into me, they can't claim they didn't notice me coming. You, however, blend into the highway in a rearview mirror."

"And you make a nice bull's-eye if they want to murder you," he pointed out.

"That's why we took your car." She smiled smugly.

"See? I'm already doing my job protecting you."

He sent her the same impish grin that used to warm her heart. Turned out it still did. They were connecting again, like old times—there was no other way of putting it.

He put the car in gear and turned his attention to driving out of the small parking garage next to his office building, but she watched his profile, unable to tear her eyes away, feeling more alive than at any time in the last six months…

What was she thinking? How easily she'd fallen back into the electric, fun banter they'd once had, as if everything was normal between them. His agreeing to help her, a little verbal football, and a whiff or two of his cologne—was that all she needed to get wrapped up again in her emotions and feelings for him? Stupid. In about an hour, maybe two, Boone was going to drop her off at her candy-orange car and they would never see each other again, unless she had an occasion to arrest someone he was defending and have to testify. And she already knew how going up against him in court worked out. No, thank you. She did not need Boone Walker–type grief.

Lord, help me to let him go. Because at this point, she wasn't sure what would be more dangerous—running into a murderous Warren Detry…or losing her heart again to Boone.

TWO

"I know you still believe Detry is guilty," Boone said after they'd pulled out onto the busy, uptown street, "so tell me. Why do you think Cliff Haggis, a cop, would hide a gun to protect a guilty man from a murder rap?"

Her warm and fuzzy feelings toward Boone fled, and her nerve endings went on red alert. That had to be the quickest answer to a prayer she'd ever had. She hadn't wanted to feel a connection to Boone again, but she also hadn't wanted this irritation at him washing through her. She'd rather not be feeling anything for him at all.

"You're trying to argue again," she pointed out.

"I'm a lawyer," he said with a charming smile. "Arguing is what I do."

She sighed. "Can't you just be my bodyguard and let me take care of the business end?"

"If I have to shoot somebody, that *is* the business end. The more knowledge I have about what's going on, the better chance I'll have of not picking off an innocent man."

True. She took a deep breath. "I don't know why Cliff hid the evidence. Maybe he knew Detry from someplace and owed him a big favor. Or maybe Detry offered a bribe to hide it and Cliff desperately needed money."

"Or maybe Cliff hid the weapon because he killed Detry's wife himself."

She was wrong. Warm and fuzzy *was* preferable to wanting to box Boone's ears in. "Get real," she denied flatly. "I told you already, Cliff couldn't commit cold-blooded murder."

"Anyone could, given the right circumstances. Like right now, you look like you want to kill me."

"That would be justifiable homicide, not murder."

The boyish grin, so out of sync with his rugged, dark features, returned. She couldn't help herself, she slowly grinned back. They both knew she didn't mean it, about wanting him dead. And smiling at Boone didn't mean she was any less irritated with him.

Did it?

"Cliff's wife said they didn't know the victim, and I believe her," she said, preferring the arguing to examining how she was honestly feeling. "Detry killed his wife with the missing weapon, and I believe what we find is going to prove it. And the new evidence might just stand up in court, because no way a cop is planting Detry's fingerprints on it to frame him, but then burying the weapon. That doesn't make sense."

"Look, Angie, they found no other evidence against Detry anywhere. So why are you so sure you're going to find usable prints?"

"I just am."

Boone shook his head, but Angie let the argument go, gazing out the window at the large city park they were passing, with its trees and walking trails. She actually had a lot of reasons for thinking Detry had murdered his wife, and they were all good.

The first reason stemmed from something that had occurred at the scene of the crime. She'd arrived soon after Cliff that afternoon at the Detry mansion in response to the 911 call reporting a murder. She'd checked the victim's cold body and spotted what she presumed was the murder weapon several feet away. She had to help Cliff secure the huge place, so she didn't remain there. In the next room, she'd found Detry, sitting with his face in his hands. The early middle-aged man, a total stranger, had looked at her, and his expression had changed from grief to surprise—and then to a coldness that had left a permanent chill in her. Before they could exchange words, Cliff had found them and given her rooms to search. Later, Detry metamorphosed back into the grieving husband, but Angie had walked away that day convinced he was guilty.

Another reason for still doubting Detry's innocence was the e-mail she'd gotten a week after his acquittal that said, simply, "I will not forgive you." She'd had it traced by the Ohio Bureau of Criminal Investigation's computer division to a nearby library, but they'd never located the person who'd sent it.

And finally, there was Angie's sister. Detry had gotten involved with a church's Reach Out to Prisoners program while incarcerated to await trial and claimed to have found God. What he'd also found was her sister, Chloe, who was involved in the ministry. If that had been their only connection, it would have been a coincidence, sure. But not a month after Detry had been found not guilty, he'd tracked down and begun dating Chloe. Out of the blue, Chloe had called Angie up to forgive her for a past wrong and to try to reconcile—because Warren Detry had asked her to.

Angie shivered. She figured Detry was dating Chloe for revenge on her, since she'd refused to back down in court about having seen the presumed murder weapon. The man was evil, and she was not waiting around until he decided he would get his ultimate revenge on her—killing her sister. She was fighting him now with all she had in her.

Gut instinct, that's how she knew the prints would point to

Detry. But Boone didn't trust instinct or feelings. He dealt in hard evidence. That was fine. She had a fact for him.

"I'll give you one reason I'm sure about Detry's guilt," she told him finally, when they'd come to the outskirts of Copper City and were riding down a highway studded with ranch homes. "The insurance policy on his wife was for half a mil. That always screams husband."

Boone shook his head. "Not this time."

"Why do you say that?"

"The insurance broker said the wife was the one who took out the policy, not Detry. He even remembered her saying her husband wasn't going to like it, but she wanted him to have money to keep up the house if she died."

"A house he promptly sold after he was acquitted. You don't think he influenced her at all?" she asked skeptically.

His look said "you know what I think already."

How exasperating could one man get? "I can't wait till we get a print match."

"Me, neither." He grinned like that would make him the happiest man on earth.

Since she was afraid she would say something that would get Boone talking about the relationship they didn't have, she concentrated on watching the highway behind them for signs they were being followed. Boone also kept silent, for which she was grateful.

A few minutes later, they passed under the gateway arch at the cemetery and parked in front of a small building toward the front that resembled a homey cottage more than a place of business. Tiny flowers in various shades of pink and red growing in window boxes brightened the front, and a sign that read "Last Stop" in flowing script hung over the door.

Boone and Angie got out and scanned the area around them.

"No cars, no one lurking around the trees," she observed. "No one followed us, either. We've been lucky."

"It's too quiet," Boone said. "Dead quiet."

"I am *not* walking down that pun trail," she told him, swinging her shoulder bag from her side to her hands to dig for her badge and ID.

"I wasn't trying to be funny. Somebody threatened you with death if you don't forget about the Detry murder, which remains unsolved, with a murderer still out there—"

She opened her mouth to protest, but Boone narrowed his eyes, and she gave up, preferring to pick her battles.

"But there's not so much as a hint of anything out of place on the trip over, or here." He shook his head. "Something's not right."

"We took *your* car so no one would spot us. Maybe we're just doing everything right."

"Or maybe the danger isn't who or what you think it is."

"Boone, please go back to doing funny. I like you better that way." She found what she needed to prove she was a cop to the caretaker and zipped her bag closed.

"Right. We can joke. Just don't discuss anything serious, right?"

"You're not talking about Detry now, are you?" She met him eye to eye and knew she was correct. His grim look was back. That warning, knowing stare that convinced jurors he was right and won court cases—but wouldn't win her.

Sighing, she started toward the door of the caretaker's cottage office, not caring if Boone followed or not.

Her cell phone rang before she got halfway up the walk. She slipped her badge and ID inside one pocket of her beige, cropped jacket and grabbed the phone out of the other. Her sister's number showed in the little window.

Angie's heart thumped against her chest. This call was not to chat. Chloe didn't "chat" with her. They were both still too bruised and cautious about their renewed relationship, which was another reason she wasn't jumping into the middle of her sister's romance with her gun drawn on Detry. She knew who Chloe would side with.

The phone kept chirping. She turned around to find Boone staring at her curiously. He was still by his Mercedes.

"I have to get this," she more asked than said.

Boone shrugged his broad shoulders, and she tried to convince herself she didn't want to hide her face against one now. She never hid from anything, but she did not want to take this call. What on earth was wrong with her?

She was afraid of what Chloe was going to say, that was what.

With a deep breath, she walked well away from Boone to the back of his car, hit a key on the phone and cupped her hand over her mouth to keep her voice from carrying. She hoped.

"Chloe?"

"Ange, yes, it's me. I have the greatest news, and I just had to call you. I hope that's okay. You said the other night you would get this week off, right?"

"Right." She'd called Chloe the night she'd found Cliff dead, unnerved by shock, wanting to make sure her sister was still all right. Maybe she'd also called Chloe because she wanted to hear the voice of someone familiar. It hadn't comforted her, not when she'd really wanted to be talking to…someone else. She glanced at Boone.

"Chief Gregg gave me over a week of compassionate leave time," Angie added. To pull herself together, which she would have to do all over again when she attended the funeral tomorrow. Nine days to get over losing a friend. It wouldn't be enough. She already knew that.

She needed to focus on her sister. Chloe was chatting and gushing. Chloe sounded extremely happy. And given the circumstances of her sister's life at the moment, that could only mean one thing.

"Warren proposed!" Chloe chirped in her ear. "We're getting married Saturday."

Oh, please, Lord, no, was what she thought. "Wow," was what she said. What else could she say?

"I'm so happy," Chloe added. "I was going to let you get the invitation in the mail, but Warren said he'd imagine a call would surprise you more."

Oh, yeah. Angie rested her hips against Boone's car, her knees threatening mutiny. Detry was a snake coiling around her neck. Tightly.

She couldn't tell Chloe her suspicions yet. She needed absolute proof to back her up, like that murder weapon, with only Detry's fingerprints on it. She probably could use more than that—maybe an indicting tidbit from Detry's past that Boone missed when he ran the man's background check. And hard as it was for her to accept, she probably needed to ask Boone to let her read his copy of that report. Detry was already making his moves. There was no time to waste.

As her sister bubbled over with hopes and dreams for her future with a murderer, Angie cast a long look at Boone. How on earth would she get him to go along with her game plan of ruining his former client, which would require his admitting to having made a mistake?

Around them birds chirped; an elderly woman, with a waterfall of red roses next to her, drove through the gate; and a plane flew through some clouds overhead. So much for the dead quiet. The world was back to normal—except for her own life.

"Ange, I really want you to be there for the shower, the rehearsal and the wedding. There's a party, too, one evening. Mom said you can stay at the house if you don't want to drive back and forth." Some of the gush left Chloe's voice as she added, "If you can come soon, maybe it will give us some time together to get to know each other again before I'm all caught up with being a wife. I'd like that."

"I'd like that, too," Angie whispered. She refused to tear up now, with Boone's intense gaze on her. "I do love you, Chloe." She couldn't remember the last time she'd said that—if she ever had. She must have, right?

At the other end of the invisible line, Chloe hesitated, a reflection of the hard times they'd had. "I love you, too. My invitation will have the dates and times. Please let us know when you're coming. Bye!" She disconnected.

Angie slipped her phone back into her pocket and straightened up. Boone moved to her side, so close their arms were touching. She longed to lean into him and absorb some of his strength. He was always a rock, no matter what, and she'd been on her own so long that leaning on him held great appeal. She ought to be thinking of God as her rock, but sometimes, like now when trouble was slapping her into a small, dark place, God seemed so remote.

"You hear my heart, Boone?"

"Is this a test?" he asked lightly.

"I'm surprised you can't hear my heart," she said, not joking. Her sister's situation was life or death. She pulled her bag up into her arms to hold that instead of him. "*I* can hear my heart. It's pounding."

"You're upset."

"Yeah, I guess." Whether or not now was a good time to ask him for permission to read the background check he'd done on Detry, she wasn't certain. She doubted if he would let her if she didn't first tell him about her sister's engagement and how she was going to stop the wedding. Was it a good idea? She needed to think, but Boone's intense gaze and nearness made that extremely difficult.

"Bad news?" Boone asked.

"Yes, I would say so." She backed away from him a little to break the mental hold he had on her. "That was my sister."

Boone's face registered surprise. "I thought you two weren't speaking."

"We weren't, until Warren Detry stepped into the picture. Chloe was part of a Bible study ministry for inmates. That's how they met. When he was freed, he looked her up at her church, and they started dating."

"You were going to tell me this when?" His eyes narrowed.

"Now?" She lifted her eyebrow. The edges of his lips lifted, but only briefly. His attention was diverted by the elderly lady's car leaving. He watched the vehicle carefully, then resettled himself to look at her.

"Go on," he said.

"Chloe never believed Detry capable of murder. At some point, Warren discovered we were sisters. Not too long ago, he made it a point to 'encourage' Chloe to reconcile with me." Not out of any love of his fellow man, Angie was certain. The monster just wanted to assure she was out there, scared. Sweating. Petrified.

"The call just now was to tell me she and Warren are getting married Saturday." She met Boone's eyes again. "*Warren* encouraged her to call and invite me especially. He's taunting me."

"Angie—"

"He *is*," she insisted, "because I know as soon as Chloe moves in with him, she's readily available to be his next victim, and he wants me to worry. He must know we're here, looking for the evidence. That I'm not giving up, despite his death threat on my car this morning. He'll either kill her to get revenge on me for insisting the murder weapon existed, or he'll hold her over my head to keep me from taking the murder weapon to the authorities."

Boone's skeptical eyes made Angie want to kick him in the shins, but she held back. At the rate today was going, she would probably just break a toe. Besides, she was trying to change inside, to mature as a Christian.

A hard battle, especially when it came to Boone, in more ways than one.

"I'll admit," Boone said, "that his choosing your sister to fall in love with and marry is very coincidental, but it's not like he went looking to meet her in the first place just to get revenge on you. The trial hadn't even happened yet when they met."

Was she wrong? The memory of Detry's evil eyes lacerating her appeared in her mind like fireworks, clear and sharp at first, then fading into nothingness, and she shivered, despite the warmth of the June morning. No, she wasn't wrong. She'd met up with perps like him before, men who had it out for females, but never any with the intensity of hatred in their eyes that Detry had displayed toward her. Her guess was that Detry was a psychopath who hated women. When she'd claimed a weapon existed that he'd stated wasn't there, she'd become tops on his hit list.

Maybe it had been a coincidence Detry met Chloe, and maybe even that he'd found out they were sisters. But it hadn't been by chance he'd sought out Chloe later, after the trial was over, and begun dating her. No, that had been his plan.

But she'd never convince Boone of that.

"You're also assuming Detry was guilty," he added, "and that someone else didn't commit Laurie Detry's murder and write that note to you. Someone who doesn't want the weapon found now."

She sidestepped impatiently. "Do I really need to remind you there were no signs of any break-in or struggle at the mansion?

That the forensics team found no stranger's prints anywhere? I'd stake my life on there not being an intruder."

"I wouldn't stake your life on that," Boone said fiercely.

That almost sounded like he cared. She supposed he did, in a way, but he cared more about his clients. He would never side with her over one of them. Ever. This was proving it. Worse, he was gazing down at her as though she were being an illogical child. Just like at the trial, he was still doubting her opinions and abilities. That hurt.

No matter what he thought, Detry was dangerous, and she believed that to the depths of her soul. Because he'd put Chloe up to this latest call, Angie was almost positive he wasn't planning to murder her anytime soon. He would have too much fun getting his revenge by watching Angie squirm…while the clock ticked away the seconds till his next murder.

Her sister's.

So physically, Angie was safe—for now. Mentally, though, she knew Boone would fight her the whole way on breaking up Detry and her sister, and he was a formidable enemy to have. She needed to stay on his friendly side until she got the information about Detry she wanted.

"Tell you what. Since there's no danger, and we seem to waste a lot of time disagreeing with each other on this, I'm demoting you from bodyguard back to lawyer."

To say Boone looked shocked would be an understatement. "You sure you want to do that, Angel?"

Hearing his nickname for her brought back memories that made her warm inside. He'd called her Angel all the time when they were together. She wished she could tell him to stop now, but if she did, he might think she was still bitter toward him. She was, and maybe he even knew she was, but if he didn't, she didn't want him to figure it out. She wanted him to think "help Angie."

She kept her voice even. "I know you've been enjoying your elevation in status, but you can go back to your office, and I'll take a cab there with the evidence when I'm done."

"What makes you think I would just leave you here?"

"Because there's no reason for you to stay." Distracted by the movement of curtains in the cottage window, she paused. They needed to hurry up before someone got worried and called the police. That would be messy. Chief Gregg would not be pleased if she became the center of attention—again.

"The way I figure it, before he died, Cliff must have let Detry know that he told me that he'd buried the evidence, but not where exactly. I don't know why Cliff would have done that, but that's what I think happened." She gave Boone a few seconds to process that. "So Detry, angry, decided to threaten me with the note. Not because he has plans to kill me. That's no real fun when it comes to revenge. No, he'll get his jollies from me panicking."

"You don't know any of this for certain."

"He had Chloe call me to announce the wedding, Boone," she repeated. "He was turning his knife in my gut. He's totally aware my sister and mother are all I've got now that he tore you and me apart."

Much to her dismay, Boone's relaxed aura was gone, and he straightened, looking critically at her. "That's the whole problem you have with him, isn't it? We might still be together if I hadn't taken him on as a client."

"No, Detry is the whole problem I have with *you*. That you chose him to defend—and not me." The burning behind her eyes started, and Angie knew she needed to get mad instead of cry. She'd done enough crying over her past already, before and after Boone. "Besides, we wouldn't have lasted even without Detry. There are too many differences between us. But that doesn't matter now. I need to make my sister understand he is dangerous—

that's what does matter to me. Not putting him in prison—and not you."

Her words were like a gut punch. Boone turned away from her and scanned the trees and road, determined to focus on watching out for threats. But one thought lingered on his mind like fire licking at a log—he no longer mattered to her.

"So I don't need you to watch my back any longer."

"I think you do." She had tunnel vision where Detry was concerned and would never accept that he was innocent, and she could still be in danger from sources unknown. Not good. She needed him and couldn't even see it. Or refused to, because he'd hurt her.

Whatever she said, he wasn't leaving her there alone. He was finally there for her, one hundred percent there, but he feared it was too late.

"Don't risk your life just because you're angry with me," he said. "I think someone else wrote the note for some other reason, and you're still in immediate danger—maybe more than you think."

"You're wrong," she said, her eyes flashing furiously.

"I am?"

"You've been wrong before."

In court, about her, she meant. Boone knew she was right. He considered apologizing, not for choosing to defend his client over her, but for thinking there were no other possibilities for the evidence having disappeared beyond her being negligent.

That the gun could have been purposely hidden had never occurred to him. Cliff Haggis, the first responder the night of the murder from the small, understaffed, Copper City PD, was a decorated, well-respected police detective. He'd testified he had not seen the weapon Angie had described. Likewise, there was no reason to believe the crime-scene investigation team, called in from nearby Cincinnati, would have any reason to thwart the murder investigation. The only possibility he'd come up with was that Angie had somehow missed the real perp inside the mansion, who had taken the weapon at some point and fled unnoticed before the rest had shown up.

He'd played the case the way he needed to in order to free an innocent man, and he couldn't apologize for that.

"Okay, so I was wrong—once," he admitted. "That doesn't mean I'm wrong now. Making faulty assumptions about someone's guilt could get you killed."

"There's steam coming out of my ears, Boone."

As determined as she was not to listen to him, he was just as determined to protect her. "How about if I keep my opinions to myself and tag along with you anyway?" he asked.

"Why would you want to?"

Boone considered his answer carefully. Because he owed her. Because he thought she was wrong about the threat to her life and didn't want her to be dead wrong. Because…

"Because I missed you."

Her cheeks flushed pink. "Quit saying that!"

He shrugged. "Can't help it."

"And don't be charming."

"Me? I don't know the meaning of the word." He grinned, because he was getting through to her. He could tell. "I'm just trying to make you happy."

Angie, exasperated, waved her hand in the air. "Never mind. Tag along if you want to, while I dig up the gun, but don't talk to me."

"Even if I see danger?"

"You're causing me to have premature aging lines," she told him.

"See? Even when I'm the exact way you want me to be, you're not happy."

He might be right about that, and what did that say about her?

"I'm not talking to you anymore." Leaving Boone behind,

Angie walked up the concrete sidewalk to the cottage, where she rapped once on the door to announce her arrival and entered.

A woman in her late sixties with frosted, dark blond hair and weathered skin sat behind the desk inside reading a best-seller Angie recognized based on a real serial killer. In a cemetery. Gutsy.

The woman met her eyes with some emotion in hers that came and went quickly, spooking Angie. Then her face took on a world-weariness that held a hint of amusement.

"Took you long enough to get in here," the woman said, laying her novel carefully on the side of her desk and joining Angie at the counter. "I watched you two for a while, but then I got bored. Too much conflict, not enough resolution."

Uncanny how that about nailed down her entire life, Angie thought.

"You and that fella married?"

"No," Angie said firmly, ignoring the giant moth trying to take off in the pit of her stomach. "Never."

"Good thing. You'd be a divorce waiting to happen."

Wow, if outsiders could tell, she'd done the right thing disengaging herself from Boone. Or trying to, anyway. The door shut behind her and she sensed Boone right back at her side. Close. Very close.

She elbowed him. It was like hitting concrete. He backed off, and she turned her attention to the cemetery's caretaker. The nameplate on the front counter said she was Ida Zlotsky.

"Ida, I have a problem." Leaving out as much information as she could, Angie explained who she was and what she wanted to do, including the part about digging up possible evidence. Ida gazed unabashedly at Boone the whole time. Angie wondered if she'd even listened, but then Ida spoke without looking at her.

"Whose grave?"

"Laurie Detry's."

With a hard blink, Ida turned her attention from Boone to her—another strange reaction, Angie thought. But since the woman wasn't saying no, she didn't challenge her on it, just presented her ID and badge.

Ida checked both with half an eye, then returned her attention to Boone. "He a cop, too?" she asked with a wide smile at him.

"No," Angie and Boone both said together, only Boone's "no" sounded more like "no way, never." Angie gave him a long-suffering look and put her identification away in her bag.

"That was too quick," Ida said. "What, is he undercover or something? A rogue cop? 'Cause you look just like that rogue cop on that forensics show a couple seasons ago, the one who got killed—"

The very thought of Boone dying hit too close to home and made Angie cringe. Apparently some part of her wasn't that mad at him. Go figure.

"I'm a criminal-defense lawyer," Boone said. "I'm here to keep her out of jail."

Angie thrust her thumb backward toward Boone. "And I'm pretending he's not here."

Ida's pale green eyes lit up. Good thing someone was finding the whole situation funny, Angie thought, because she was nearing the edge of her patience.

"Now, Ida, have you noticed anything happening around here lately you might consider weird?"

"Yeah." Ida nodded seriously. "You two."

"You walked right into that one, Angie." Boone chuckled.

"I'll take that as a no." Angie said to the woman. She threw a steely-eyed, "please be quiet" expression over her shoulder at Boone, then turned back to the caretaker. "So would it be all right if we looked for that evidence at the gravesite?"

Ida pushed back wayward bangs from her eyes and grinned from ear to ear. "Have at it. I'll even look it up on our map and save you the trouble of finding it."

"Excellent."

"As long as I can watch what you're doing."

Angie sighed. This was just not her day. Not her week. If her sister's life wasn't hanging by a thread, she would cash in her metal detector and go home. "It's police business," she said, trying to dissuade the clerk and hoping the woman didn't decide to call the precinct. "Could be dangerous."

"Honey, I used to work in a biker bar. I can handle danger."

"I might need Ida's help," Boone said. Angie shot him with her eyes, but he chose not to shut up. "She probably has self-defense tricks up her sleeve I never thought of."

"You betcha," Ida said, winking at him. "Honey, if you don't want this eye magnet, I'd like a crack at him."

"Have at it," Angie said, rolling her eyes at Boone's grin. Ida didn't notice—she was too busy gazing at Boone.

"You sure you're a lawyer?" she asked him. "'Cause I think you look like one of those handsome mobsters in the movies."

Lawyer or mobster? Too good to resist, even considering she had taken a vow of silence where Boone was concerned. Turning, Angie opened her mouth, but Boone's fingers suddenly covered her lips to shush her.

"Don't even start," he warned, his dark eyebrows slanting.

She couldn't speak anyway. The last thing she'd expected was his touching her—or the joy flooding her from the contact.

She stared up at him, confused, and to her amazement, he looked just as startled as she did. But she wasn't the reason. Turning, she followed his gaze.

Ida stood there, holding a gun in her hand.

Splitting apart to opposite sides of the room like they had been working together for years, Angie and Boone simultaneously drew their own weapons, ready for a stand-off.

THREE

"Relax. I was just holding it up to show you two I had it. I wasn't going to shoot the thing." Ida's wrinkles grew even deeper as she gingerly put the gun down on the counter. "If you two don't beat all. Saying how dangerous what you're here to do is, and then spending time making goo-goo eyes at each other so you don't even notice someone has a gun until they could have shot you."

"She has a point, Angie," Boone said, moving his jacket to holster his Glock. "Better stop making goo-goo eyes at me. You're too distracting."

Like she needed this? Angie scowled at the other woman. "I did not make goo-goo eyes at Boone."

Ida just smiled at Boone, who gave her that boyish grin Angie thought he kept reserved for her. So much for thinking she was special. With a fast sigh, Angie reholstered her own weapon at her ankle and checked Ida's. "It's loaded."

"Of course it is. What good would an empty gun be?"

She liked the logic. The woman reminded her a lot of herself, and Angie wasn't sure if she liked that or not. She returned the weapon to Ida. "Better put it back wherever you keep it."

"Sure," Ida said. A few seconds later, the firearm was safely locked inside a steel counter drawer. "I only got it out because you said digging up what you're after could be dangerous. But

I should have figured you'd both be carrying already. I'll be safe enough, I guess."

Angie bit her tongue to keep from asking Ida if she had a permit for the weapon, because if the caretaker didn't, then she would have to do something about it, and she didn't need further delays. She could also have asked Ida what could go on at a cemetery that would require protection, but truly, she didn't want to know.

Striding over to the door, she moved her arm in a windmill motion, gesturing for them to follow her. Outside, she took in the surrounding area, suddenly edgy again. What she was looking for, she wasn't certain. She still didn't believe Detry was coming after her right now, but Ida's suddenly brandishing a firearm had made her anxious.

As had Boone's touching her. She was still vulnerable to him, no matter how much she thought otherwise. But Boone was as much a threat to her sister's life as Detry was in a way, because Boone refused to believe her. If she fell for him all over again, she might get goo-goo-eyed for real, and let him convince her he was right, and then she would give up her mission. Chloe could end up dead.

She had to remain strong and get this done.

First things first. She needed her metal detector and shovel, but she didn't want to ask Boone for any favors. So she merely pointed to his trunk.

"Aren't you being just a bit childish with this 'no talk' thing?" Boone asked, getting his keys out.

Probably, but she didn't care. The less contact she had with him, the less she would think about him. But she wasn't telling him that. Retrieving her tools, she saw Ida smile from ear to ear, and she lifted her eyebrows at her in question. "Something amusing you?"

"You two. You're more fun than a soap opera." Ida waved her

hand in a northerly direction and set the pace, telling them Laurie Detry's grave was a thousand feet or so from the office building.

"So, Ida, what was it like working in a biker bar?" Boone asked.

That was all the encouragement the older woman needed. In the next five minutes, Angie learned more about Ida Zlotsky than she'd ever imagined possible. Years ago, her husband had walked out on her, she'd had two babies to support, and no car, and waitressing at the biker bar was the only work within walking distance.

"I thought I was going to die when he left," Ida said. "But I got my act together, and I made it."

"I understand that," Boone said. "My mom was in about the same situation when I was a kid. When she got married, she thought she would be able to stay home and raise me, but it didn't happen that way, and she wound up working two jobs. It was rough."

He asked Ida another question, but Angie stopped listening. Boone had gone through a really bad childhood, just like her? He'd never told her. And this caring side of him where Ida was concerned—she'd never seen it with anyone other than herself. He seemed genuinely interested in the caretaker as a person and not just in passing time till they got to the grave.

Her eyes sweeping the area, Angie listened to Ida talking about how she'd learned to make a mean tequila sunrise at the bar, and also how to swing a baseball bat effectively—at two bikers who just wouldn't stop fighting. She'd also never gotten held up.

"The bikers watched over me."

God had watched over her, Angie immediately thought. She knew she ought to tell Ida that, and would have before Cliff's death. But now, doubt held her tongue captive. If God *was* watching over believers, He had to have been watching over Cliff. So what had happened? Cliff had told her many times he had great faith in God's seeing him through his problems. So how did he get to the point of suicide?

No, she couldn't say a thing to Ida. She still believed in God, but she was no longer so certain of the answers that she wanted to jump into leading people like Ida to Him—if Ida indeed was an unbeliever. What if the cemetery caretaker had questions that she just couldn't answer—like she herself had about Cliff? Anything she might say, including doubts, might turn the woman away from God. So Angie kept quiet, feeling guilty for doing so.

"When he was young, my son didn't like his mother working in a bar. He was gonna be somebody, and he didn't want people thinking he came from the wrong side of the tracks."

"Boy, do I understand that."

Boone's simple, earnest words got to Angie, and her heart went out to him.

"My daughter complained people at school called her trash because I worked there. But I stayed, because it brought in good money and kept a roof over their heads. In the long run, it didn't matter anyway. My son ended up in jail, and my daughter—she died. I'm all alone."

Angie's heart clenched again, this time for Ida. She met the other woman's eyes. Really looked at her—and saw the same pain she'd seen reflected in her own many times. "I'm sorry. I know how hard it is to not have anyone."

Ida nodded.

"Belonging to a church helped me. It's like having family around." The next closest thing, especially when the family you'd been born into hated you. "We're having a bring-a-dish lunch after services Sunday. Lots of ladies your age to talk to, if you're interested."

Ida waved her hand through the air. "I'd never fit in with church people. I'm not that good."

"Don't worry, neither am I," Angie assured her.

"I actually loved church when I was a kid," Boone said out of the blue.

Angie turned to look at him, frowning. The eccentric caretaker was getting more information out of Boone about his childhood than she'd ever managed to. Had she really been the right person for him, or had she just been fooling herself?

Boone added, "But I'll never go back."

"Why not?" Ida asked.

At first, Boone hesitated, but then he shrugged as they followed the access road past a couple of rows of gravesites. "Unfortunately, those nice, friendly church people soured when my dad got falsely accused of a crime and went away, and my mother couldn't afford to meet her tithe. They asked her if she'd like to be taken off the membership rolls, and she accepted. We never went back."

"That's why I don't go." Ida sniffed. "Hypocrisy."

"I agree—except for Angie," Boone said. "You can trust her totally."

"Oh, no, Ida, now I'm going to have to like the guy again," Angie joked to cover up the flood of compassion Boone's story had started in her. Even though she wasn't looking at him, she sensed his gaze on her again, and she sucked in her breath to stop herself from telling him how sorry she was about his childhood and his father, and the church people. How she wished she could change his life for him. How she wished she could make everything right between them and overlook their differences because she needed to love and be loved.

Just like her sister was overlooking everything scary about Detry because of *her* needs. The realization brought Angie up short, but before she could explore it further, Ida stopped and pointed down a long row of graves.

"The Detry one is at the end."

Boone followed Ida down the wide path, his dark blue gaze constantly watching everything around them, and Angie followed him. Ida stopped at a lavish gravestone with the engraving *"To My Darling Wife. I never stopped loving you."*

Love as in two holes in his wife's forehead. Angie's skin crawled. Detry terrified her. That could be dangerous, because she needed to keep her wits about her. *Lord, help me not to be afraid.*

This is not about you, she thought.

Lord, please help me save my sister from him.

That was better—she felt a peace about that. Scanning the ground in the front and rear of the stone for signs of recent digging, she ended up disappointed. Nothing but nicely trimmed grass that colored the ground a rich green everywhere. Upkeep charges on the grave must run a fortune. *What a man, that Warren Detry.*

"At least we know where some of the insurance money went." A lavish gravesite and romancing her sister, who liked nice, expensive things after growing up poor. Angie's thoughts went back to her earlier realization about Chloe's overlooking Detry's past and that he was almost old enough to be her father. Her sister had always had a passion for money, which apparently Detry had, in spades. Detry could take care of her.

Yeah, like he took care of Laurie Detry.

Not that she was harping on Chloe. Angie rotated the power knob on the metal detector to On and swept it over the ground around the grave. She understood her sister's need for money. It represented security. Her own passion had been finding love— that was her form of security. Love was something she'd sorely missed growing up and meant everything to her. Used to be, she'd do anything to get love.

But now, her focus was turned to Christ, and she was pursuing a relationship with Him and letting God supply the love and security. Only with Boone so close, her inclination was to forget all that and fall into his arms. It would be so easy.

Trying to forget what she wanted to do, she concentrated on what she needed to do and frowned at the expanse of grass around the gravestone. The gauge hadn't budged. A wave of disappointment hit her. Maybe Cliff's words about letting the dead rest in peace hadn't been a word puzzle, but rather, an instruction to her, and he'd hidden the evidence somewhere else. If only there was some way of knowing for sure that he hadn't buried it somewhere around the cemetery…

Her eyes darted up, surveyed the area, and she spotted a camera in a nearby oak. She was right. Spycams.

"Ida, do you have access to the surveillance footage?" she asked, pointing toward the tree.

Ida shifted position, as she took in the camera, and she shook her head. "Those are only up for show to scare off the juvenile delinquents."

Disappointed, Angie turned toward Boone. He had walked from the graves to the chain-link fence that bordered the east side of the cemetery, his dark gaze studying everything but her. She'd have to break her vow of silence to him after all.

"Apparently, I was wrong," she said in his general direction. He still didn't look at her.

She carried the metal detector the dozen or so yards to where he was, and repeated, with a spread of her arms to emphasize she was speaking, "Apparently, I was wrong, *Boone*."

A light squeal erupted from the detector, and startled, Angie almost dropped it. She stared down at the search coil at the bottom of the rod, and the cluster of marigolds near it.

Boone did likewise. She stepped closer to him. Right over the single cluster of candy-orange marigolds in the line of yellow ones, the squeal became louder and the gauge stick shot up.

"That's either your evidence, or you've found buried treasure," Ida said from behind them.

"In this case, maybe both," Angie said.

Boone saw the light in Angie's eyes. If she'd found the missing murder weapon and by some remote possibility Detry's prints *were* on it in a manner that proved murder, that meant he had been wrong and had been directly responsible for a murderer going free. A mistake like that was inexcusable—not to mention what he'd done to Angie in court.

On the other hand, he was not looking forward to what was more likely to happen—someone else's prints being found on the gun—maybe even Cliff's. That would take all the light right back out of Angie's eyes.

Either way, he almost wished the evidence could stay buried. He simply could not be wrong, and he didn't want Angie hurt all over again.

The squeal was maxed out, so Angie turned off the metal detector. The sudden silence was velvet to her ears.

"Cliff must have picked those flowers specifically so you would notice them," Boone said. He turned to Ida and explained in a manner that fully invited her sympathizing with him, "She has a car painted the same orange that's on candy corn."

For a change, instead of agreeing with Boone, Ida smiled at Angie. "Nice choice. At least other drivers can't claim they didn't see you coming."

"Ida, I'm beginning to like you a lot," Angie said. Boone shook his head in mock disgust, and she went back to looking at the flowers. The candy-orange flowers were smaller than the others, another tip-off they'd been planted later. Cliff had to have purposely dug up the site and replanted with those to get her attention. It was time to dig.

Pulling a camera from her purse, Angie checked the film and

snapped a couple of pictures, then placed everything she carried except the shovel on the ground, making sure the camera was accessible.

With latex gloves ready nearby from the supply she brought with her, just in case she was successful today, she dug, stopping from time to time to document the uncovering of evidence with her camera. The wind that was supposed to bring in forecasted thunderstorms picked up, cooling her off some as she worked her muscles.

After a while, she glanced up at Boone. His eyes were sweeping the perimeter of the cemetery as he continued to protect her from an enemy he still considered unknown. As irritating as it was that he wouldn't believe her about the danger being nil right then, that Boone cared enough to still be there no matter what kind of fire she set at his feet took just a bit of the hurt in her heart away.

A few minutes later, she unearthed the weapon, a Colt Model 1911, .45 caliber, semi-automatic pistol, a match to the bullets recovered and to the antique gun she'd seen near the body. It was in a sealed evidence bag along with the chain of custody form, which had only one name written on it—Cliff's.

The murder weapon.

Ida's whole face was puckered up, reflecting the "eeew" factor of reality murder that never could quite come through in suspense novels. "There's dried blood on that thing, isn't there?"

Blood, and Angie didn't want to think about what else as she put on her gloves.

"Don't detectives use evidence boxes for weapons now?" Boone asked her.

She started to speculate that maybe the bag was all Cliff had handy when he stole it from the scene, but Ida was right there, watching both of them like she was getting paid to do so, so Angie only shrugged, not wanting to give away too much information. Holding the bag by one corner, she carefully placed it into an empty compartment in her oversized purse, specks of dirt and all, and started to push the soil back into the hole with her shovel.

"Don't worry about that," Boone told her, taking a couple of bills out of his wallet. Angie stopped and watched him give the money to Ida. "This should cover replacing the flowers."

Ida's eyes went big. "Sure thing," she said. "You leave me your business card, and I'll be happy to send you the change."

"Keep it," Boone said.

Ida beamed. "You two have been fun, but I gotta get back so I can get a hold of the landscaper before someone sees the mess and has their serenity interrupted. If you need more help, just whistle." Ida set off ahead of them back to the cottage.

Angie dusted off the knees of her jeans and then peeled off her gloves. With Ida gone, her thoughts cascaded back to Boone. She shouldn't ask him about the money. She shouldn't. But in the last half hour or so, she had witnessed a new, vulnerable side of him she hadn't known existed, giving her a smidgen of hope he had it in him to change from the work-possessed person he was into someone who might really put her first. She had to find out. "What was with the handout?"

"She reminded me of my mother," he said. "Always struggling, never coming out ahead, and never quite being noticed by anyone. So I noticed her." He shrugged like it was no big deal.

"You never told *me* that much about your childhood."

Every muscle of his body stiffened. She had to remember she no longer had any right to challenge him on anything he did. They weren't in love anymore. They weren't anything anymore, not even good friends.

"Sorry," she said. "I shouldn't have asked."

His expression said he agreed with her, but then he spoke

anyway. "Dad was wrongly accused of murder, got convicted and died in prison before I got my law degree and could help him. It was hard for Mom before I got old enough to work. I don't like to talk about it."

Bending, he scooped up the metal detector and the shovel and waited for her to start walking back. She did, stepping ahead, but she sensed him keeping up behind her. So close, she couldn't avoid thinking about him.

His father's misfortune explained a lot about Boone. Just like her and her sister, he was driven by a passion—he was freeing his dad with every man he defended. Now she understood why he'd chosen Detry over her. Problem was, understanding only lessened the pain a little; it didn't take it all away. Didn't free her up to fall back in love with him.

She walked up the lane, silently, the added weight of having to part from Boone very soon now on her mind. She was no longer as irritated with him as she'd been, and the man had a magnetic pull on her that she couldn't deny. Eye magnet, as Ida had said, and maybe a heart magnet, too. She wanted him around. She wanted him to make her smile. She was so tired of frowning. Of being alone. Of not having anyone who loved her. Boone *had*. It was just that his priorities came first, and she came second.

She wanted someone to put her first.

God loves you, a small voice inside her reminded.

True. God would find her a husband who would fit into His will for her. All she had to do was wait. But she'd been waiting all her life to be really loved, and it was getting more and more difficult. Would it be better to accept Boone as he was, to settle for being second in his life? To have some love instead of none at all?

She gave herself a hard mental shake. Boone was dangerous. Being around him made her both ache with regret and wish upon a star. She couldn't afford to have her emotions swinging her mind around in circles, distracting her from the most important thing in her life—saving her sister.

A wind gust blew her hair up around her cheeks, and she glanced up at the sky. The clouds were thickening. She hoped it wasn't some sort of a sign.

"What do you say I take us right to the sheriff's department and let my friend fast-track the print identification to the criminal-investigation bureau?" Boone asked from behind her.

"Sure," she said, continuing to walk toward his car. Boone's solution would mean putting up with him awhile longer, but it also took care of her problem with explaining to the bureau herself why she wasn't filtering the gun through proper channels. She could live with that.

"So what did you have in mind while we wait for the results?" he asked.

Getting away from him. That's what she had in mind. Wait a second… "While *we* wait? It could take a couple days, we both know that. You don't have to stick around me all that time. What about your court cases?"

"I'm putting you first this time, Angel, remember?"

She sucked in a breath. That was eerie, hearing him say the exact words that had been on her mind a minute before. Eerie and sad. Some six months ago, right after the trial, she'd have been overjoyed at his statement—assuming it had been coupled with an apology. But presently, she understood what drove Boone. He was putting her first only because she'd proven him wrong about her negligence and he figured he owed her for ruining her reputation. It was more of a putting her first right now than forever kind of thing.

The big question was if she should make it easy on him to make amends or not and let him come with her to her mother's. As a Christian, she needed to forgive him. As a woman, though, her hurt was still running so very deep, and she couldn't pretend all was well between them when it definitely was not.

On the other hand, she didn't like to whine.

"What I'm going to be doing while I wait," she said, carefully keeping emotion out of her voice, "is heading to my mother's house in Newton for the wedding festivities."

"That's fine. I'll get a hotel room so I can stay close and attend all of it with you."

"There's no reason to."

"Until we figure out who threatened you, I want to be there for you. Protect you."

Make up for what he'd done, he meant. Finally reaching his Mercedes, Angie paused at the passenger's side and met his gaze over the roof. "You know I can't let this marriage happen. You're going to just sit idly by while I make your former client's life miserable by breaking up my sister and him? I don't think so."

Without waiting for his response, she opened his car door and slipped inside onto the soft seat. A few seconds later, the trunk slammed shut and the driver's side door opened. Boone slid inside minus the shovel and metal detector and started the car. The air conditioner blasted hot air at first, and she took a tissue out of her bag and wiped her forehead.

"You know, you may not have to work that hard at separating them," Boone said, causing her gaze to shift to him. "If those are Detry's prints, he could be arrested on suspicion of perjury. He'll be out of your sister's life, and the whole problem can be settled before the wedding rehearsal. You don't want to sit through that, do you?"

All the while thinking it should be her and Boone as the happy couple? You betcha, she didn't. She frowned.

"Thought not. Meanwhile, I'll be there watching your back." He smiled faintly. "Protecting you from Detry."

"Or from whoever, you mean."

He lifted his palms in surrender. "As long as nobody hurts you, Angel, I'm happy."

How could she keep from being hurt while attending the shower, the rehearsal and the dinner with Boone by her side, a constant reminder of what should have been? But she wasn't going to tell him that.

"You can just call me when the results come in," she told him. "Or better yet, just send your friend to Newton to arrest Detry." That way, her sister wouldn't blame her for ruining her happiness. As much. "I don't need you there standing up for the man with every move I make against him."

"I'm not going to betray you again, Angie, I promise." His look begged her to believe him.

She wished she could. Only she couldn't see how he could avoid it.

"I'll think about it." Averting her eyes, she slipped her tissue back into her shoulder bag and squeezed the soft leather that contained the evidence that could save her sister. Boone's heartfelt promise not to betray her again held such a nice ring, but honestly, she knew better. He would do what he had to do because that was the way he was. She dared not believe otherwise. As always, she could only count on herself.

Boone kept his eyes on the road as they drove east. The sheriff's department was about a mile on the other side of Copper City. His squared-off jaw was set in stone, and she was certain she knew why. He wanted her to say yes to his offer to come with her to the wedding. He liked being in control, dictating the moves, and she'd irritated him by making him wait.

Not only that, the talk of "wedding this" and "wedding that" might be reminding him of the two of them the way they had once been, making plans for their future, basking in the glow of being in love. Boone had really wanted to get married. So had she. The downward spiral of their relationship hadn't started until their debate over having a family had begun.

The thought of a baby tugged at her heart for a few brief seconds, but then the uncertainty stemming from her own childhood crept in once again, and she sighed. Better to concentrate on her sister's happiness, because she was beginning to doubt she'd ever have any of her own.

He sped up and turned down a road that led north of the city, toward the interstate. She frowned. "I thought our next step was getting the evidence to your friend?"

He didn't so much as glance at her, and his knuckles were white as he gripped the wheel tighter. Pins and needles of alarm broke out on her neck and spread. "Boone?"

"Hold on," he said, signaling for a left, then turning sharply again. Her body slid up against the door.

"Okay, taking the evidence to your friend isn't the next step," Angie said. "Guess two. Our next step is that you're kidnapping me?"

"Wrong." Boone gestured backward swiftly with his thumb. "Our next step is going to be losing our tail."

Before Angie could look backward, a force slammed against the back of the car. She slid forward and her seat belt grabbed, knocking the air out of her. Boone sped up. She drew a fast breath and twisted to look at whoever had just rammed Boone's pride and joy.

"Never saw them before," she breathed out.

Boone's eyes checked out the rearview. "Open the glove box, get my cell phone." He gave her a shortcut to a number to press as she undid her seat belt's strangling grip. "That's Jack Callahan's number, the Chief Deputy I told you about. Tell him what's happening, and to send us some help."

"He doesn't know me," she said, palming the phone.

"Trust me, Angie, he'll know you." For two brief seconds, Boone's royal blue eyes connected with hers. "After you left my life, I had to talk out my misery to someone. Your name, uh, came up. A lot."

Great. "You sure he's going to want to help me?" she asked, tapping on the keys.

A grin briefly graced the edges of Boone's mouth. "Probably not, but he'll want to help me."

So Boone had hurt a whole lot more over their breakup than she could ever have imagined. She wasn't sure she wanted to know that.

"What's up, Boone?" Jack answered on the other end of space.

"This is Angie Delitano, Jack. I'm with Boone going north on County Line Road. We're almost at the interstate. My life was threatened this morning, and now someone's trying to ram us. Boone says to send help."

"You in Boone's Mercedes?"

"That's right." She gave him a description of the other car, the driver and the passenger, still behind them. Getting close to ramming their bumper again.

"Tell Boone to go west on the interstate. Faster to get to you there. I'll call Highway Patrol. Don't hang up."

Angie relayed the message to Boone and then glanced backward again—the other car, a red Mustang, was almost tapping against their side. Boone's tires squealed as he took a hard left, so hard their arms almost touched. He sped down the off-ramp and merged into traffic.

"Angie, still there?"

"We're on the interstate, Jack."

"Help's coming, and I'm on my way, too. Give me a milepost number so we'll know if we're catching up."

She'd read off the second when a loud crack reverberated

through her body. The outside mirror exploded like fireworks, little pieces of silver smacking the glass window. Diving downward and shielding her face, she dropped the phone on the floor mat. Boone shoved the wheel hard to the right.

"They're shooting at us!" she said, bracing herself.

"Are you all right?" Boone asked, his eyes swinging briefly toward her. He was crouched down as much as he could be and still drive safely.

Angie flexed her fingers and wiggled her toes. "Yeah, except for the heart attack I'm having. This cannot be happening. It is not in my carefully thought-out scenario of exactly what is going on."

"I think they—" Boone quirked his thumb backward "—have their own scenario."

"And what do you think that scenario is?"

"Murder."

FOUR

Murder? Would someone honestly murder them just to get the evidence?

What was she thinking? Of course they would. People did anything they wanted to if it served their purposes. Hadn't she learned that already with Cliff? And Boone?

"You and I were keeping watch the whole time we were at the cemetery," Angie said, peering up at him. Wishing she could hold on to Boone for dear life, she gripped the console instead. "No one was around except that elderly woman visiting a grave. How on earth did we get found so easily?"

"Either there's a tracking device on this vehicle, or Ida has a big mouth."

Her head wagged. "She adored you. She wouldn't betray you."

"If the motivation's right…" Boone shot her a sideways look, and she remembered the trial. And him. And her.

"Oh, yeah."

"The question is, who did she betray us to?"

"Detry. Has to be. He wants the evidence back."

"We'll have to debate it later, Angel. Right now, looks like they're—" Boone jagged his head in a backward motion, his body still tense, his eyes never leaving the road "—gaining on us again."

Angie lifted her head high enough to peer between the seats

through the back window. They had just passed a car and were swiftly leaving it behind. She did not like going this fast as a passenger. She did not like putting her life in someone else's hands. Except maybe God's.

Yes, God's. She shut her eyes tightly to say a short prayer aloud, something she'd never done before in front of Boone. When she'd first found Christ, she'd kept her faith to herself, not wanting to drive him away. But since then she'd grown closer to the Lord, and right now, she cared more about what God thought than if Boone was bothered by her praying.

When she finished and opened her eyes, things were no better at all. Except there hadn't been another shot. Okay, that was something.

Wait a minute. They weren't totally at their pursuer's mercy. Straightening, she reached to unfasten her belt so she could move around, but Boone's hand grabbed her shoulder and urged her downward.

"Keep low."

Crack! The air split right above her and the front windshield broke. Angie jumped and screeched. If Boone hadn't kept her from rising, the glass could have been her head.

Do not fear, for I am with you. Old Testament. She wasn't sure where, but it comforted her now. Surely God wouldn't have brought her this far with the evidence if he wasn't going to keep her alive long enough to save her sister. At least, that seemed logical. But it was the only thing about this car chase that did.

Boone pushed down on the accelerator. The engine roared, and Angie's adrenaline surged. Concern for Boone, vulnerable as he was driving, overwhelmed her. She could not let Boone get hurt because someone wanted her dead. That wasn't in the training manual.

She unlocked her seat belt, yanked up her jeans' leg and pulled her weapon free from her ankle holster.

"Angie! Answer me." A masculine voice registered near her ears over the sound of her pounding heart, and she finally remembered Jack and that it might be good if she filled him in.

"They're shooting at us again, Jack," she said loudly in the direction of the phone. Then, to Boone, "Go all the way to the left lane. When you do, I'm going to shoot back through my side window. Take out a tire. That'll stop them."

Jack's protest bellowed up from the floor, but Boone's was louder. "Don't! I'm driving. You'll distract me."

"*I'll* distract you? What, the bullets flying over my head aren't already doing that?"

"It's not safe to shoot on the interstate."

"Tell *them* that." She peeked to the side of the headrest through the rear window where it wasn't cracked. The passenger aimed at her head again. "He's going to shoot." She sank as low as she could, her shock at being a victim careening toward anger.

Boone yanked the wheel to the left and passed an eighteen wheeler.

"I have to shoot. I've got to do *something* to get us out of this," she protested.

"I'm doing it. When are you going to trust me, Angie?"

If a voice could have white knuckles, his did. That couldn't be Boone speaking. Boone didn't lose control.

Ever.

"When?" he demanded again.

"When I'm sure I won't get hurt," she forced out. She swiped sweat from her forehead with her palm. His pained expression told her he understood she wasn't necessarily referring to their current circumstances. He was a definite threat to her heart, and she wasn't about to put her life totally in his hands.

"I have to do something," she added. "Prayer didn't work."

"Then pray more," he said tersely.

For a few seconds she stared at the chiseled angles of his jaw. After hearing about his past experience with religion, to pray more was the last thing she'd expected out of his mouth. Maybe God was already working in him.

One shove, and she had her weapon back in its holster. She braced herself against the console and bowed her head. Her nerves taut, she wanted to put the other hand on the gun, but she didn't. *Trust in the Lord.*

"God, I know this trouble we're in is just to make me stronger and rely more on You. That's okay. But please protect Boone from getting hurt because of me. Please don't give up on either of us, no matter how bad we flub up what You want us to do down here. Amen."

Boone cast her a lightning glance. "You didn't pray for your own safety."

"I'm working on putting others first." That included protecting Boone. She was about to draw her gun again and fire no matter what he said, but then she heard Jack calling her name.

She scooped up the phone. "Jack, sorry."

"The troopers have the Mustang spotted. Don't fire your weapon, Angie."

She repeated the news to Boone, leaving out Jack's order not to fire, and fastened her seat belt again.

"Tell him I'm not slowing down until the subject does," Boone said, slewing into the right lane. A horn blasted behind them.

Jack was fine with that. "Angie, I overheard what Boone said about trusting him."

Her face burned with embarrassment, and she almost dropped the phone. When was she going to learn to guard her tongue, anyway?

"Boone knows what he's doing," Jack said. "He saved my life in combat when we were being chased. Trust him with yours, okay?" Jack didn't wait for her to answer, just added he was getting close, and not to hang up.

She held the phone while she lifted her head high enough to look at Boone. Her heart swelled with pride for his heroism, but just as swiftly, the familiar ache was back. Boone might be Jack's hero, but he wasn't hers.

"Angie." Jack's voice sounded in her ear again. "Dispatch said the Mustang just exited the interstate. We have a couple of cruisers on them. Tell Boone he can slow down and pull over."

She did that, then straightened up and turned in her seat. Ten seconds later, she could make out the red and blue flashes from state Highway Patrol vehicles on the bridge over the interstate, going north.

It was over. For now, anyway.

Boone signaled and eased over to the shoulder. Once parked, he reached for the phone she held. While he filled Jack in, Angie leaned back in her seat, folded her arms across her chest, and tried to stop her heart from bursting through her chest. Minutes later, Boone pressed a button on the phone and pushed it into his pocket.

"Jack's going to meet us here and take your evidence in for print matching himself."

"That sounds good." Her voice was so weak she barely recognized it. She twisted around until she could see the burnt-edged hole in her headrest. That could have been her head. She felt like a puppy abandoned in the snow, shaking and helpless.

"Angel?"

She gazed at Boone. He'd come through for her, and she wanted to thank him, but her throat tightened and she couldn't speak.

"You're safe now," he said, reaching out to smooth down the tousled hair on the side of her head. His hand lingered tenderly on her cheek.

For once in her life, a sassy comeback, her best defense mechanism, failed her completely. All she could do was nod.

"Scary, huh?" He stroked her cheek gently with his fingertips. The tenderness of his touch did strange things to her resolve not to get close to him, so she lifted her hand to move his away. It shook. He noticed, his eyebrows lifting. "You can cry if you want."

"It's just the adrenaline rush," she told him. "I'm all right. And I'm not going to cry." She bit her bottom lip so she wouldn't.

"Okay."

"How about you?" she asked.

"I'm not going to cry, either." His lips parted in an easy smile.

She shook her head, but she couldn't help but smile back. Her gaze wandered over his concerned eyes, his smooth jaw and his mouth that had softened the second he'd touched her face. Not a scratch. Staring back, he leaned close and kissed her, slowly, more gently than he ever had.

And so help her, she kissed him back, lifting her hand to touch his cheek. When he pulled away, she stared steadily back at him, her eyes huge.

"Oh, Boone. We can't start up again," she said, her voice gaining strength. "It won't work."

Seconds ticked by, and he nodded. "I guess we both know that. Can I still be your bodyguard?"

"Absolutely. As long as you forget that kiss."

His lips lifted in a teasing smile. "I will if you will."

That was the trouble, she thought, lowering her hand reluctantly. She doubted she could forget. The longing for him to be her family had been rekindled, and that was a flame that was not going to easily burn out again.

Boone's cell phone started playing the theme song from *Cops,* and despite her unsettled emotions, Angie chuckled. "Let me guess. Jack."

"Don't laugh," Boone said smugly. "You should hear what song I programmed in for your number."

She pretended to grab his phone to check, but he swiveled around until he was out of range. "Jack?"

Watching him, just as she'd thought, she couldn't forget the kiss they'd just shared. She told herself it was meaningless—they'd just celebrated surviving a dangerous experience intact—that was all. To make anything more of it would be foolish, since Boone was still Boone—except that he'd told her to pray and not shoot.

That was so not Boone.

The second he put his phone away and turned to her, she saw the concern in his eyes.

"This is not a good day."

"No. Wait." She wasn't ready to go back to the danger of Detry and his murderous cohorts yet. She wanted just one more minute of talking to Boone about something other than life and death. "Honest answer, and don't think about it. Why did you tell me to pray instead of shoot?"

His eyes widened. She'd startled him. Good.

"I wanted to see how this prayer thing worked, I guess."

"And did you come to any conclusion?" she asked.

"Yes. That I should have let you shoot at the Mustang."

Her forehead furrowed in confusion. "Why? I prayed for your safety, and you weren't hurt."

"Jack told me the Mustang got away. It passed a couple of Amish buggies at top speed, which frightened the horses and caused a crash the cruisers couldn't get around. If I'd let you shoot out a tire instead of pray, maybe they'd have been caught and we'd have a chance of finding out who hired them to try to kill you."

She cupped her ear with her hand. "Did I hear correctly? Did Boone Walker just admit I was right?"

"What can I say?" He shrugged, a hint of a grin back on his lips. "Seeing you again has made me soft."

"My whole world is just awry," she said. Then her peripheral vision caught the windshield in front of her with its bullet hole, the hole that would have been in *her*, had Boone not saved her, and she sobered up.

Reality was, the men in the Mustang were still free. To kill her. This was *so* not good. Before there was one man to worry about—Detry. Now there were three. What did they want? To get the evidence before it could be turned in to the authorities? Even if guilty, Detry would never go to prison because of double jeopardy.

Unless...he'd killed someone else. But who? The only other person connected with the case who had died that she knew of was Cliff. Could Detry have had something to do with Cliff's death, thought she knew about it, and now wanted her dead before she could get him in trouble?

"Angie, tell me what you're thinking."

She raised innocent eyes to Boone. All she was sure of was that she still needed Boone to be a lookout for her, especially since she was not going to let anything stop her from separating her sister from Warren Detry.

Not even the possibility of dying.

"Maybe God gave you what you wanted," she told him.

"I'll bite," Boone said.

"You wanted to be there for me while I'm doing 'wedding week' with my family? I'm now thinking it might be best to have you along."

Boone's dark eyes lit up. "Good. I can't wait."

To see her sister married? She could. But Jack's cruiser was pulling up behind them, and she didn't want to still be discussing this in front of him. Bad enough he'd already heard what he had.

Wasting no time, Jack questioned both of them, took pictures and gathered paint chips from where the Mustang had rammed them. He also searched the Mercedes and found a tracking device. Stowing all the evidence, both from their tango with the Mustang and the Detry case, in his car, including the threatening note Angie had received and her camera, he left them with a warning they needed to get the windows fixed as soon as possible, and not to be driving around drawing trouble until they did.

Angie wished she felt better, knowing the murder weapon in the Detry case was now in safe hands, but she didn't. Her eyes scanned the road continuously as they drove away.

Despite Jack's orders, Boone pulled into a fast-food place and got them some burgers to go. For once, Boone's need to be in control was coming in handy. She was starved.

Attempted murder would do that to you.

While they waited for their burgers, Angie called her sister, who, of course, was more than happy to have Boone, the man who had saved her fiancé from a prison sentence, at her wedding. Then she called Ida, wanting to find out if Ida had seen the men in the Mustang at all. No one picked up the phone.

Same thing later, in Boone's office. She hung up in frustration. "It just keeps ringing. Not even an answering machine."

"Maybe she had to supervise somebody digging a grave for a burial this afternoon, then left and forgot to turn it on." Boone's words sounded casual, but his eyes looked as troubled as Angie felt. "Or maybe she's avoiding us because she might have been the one who alerted the Mustang in the first place, and hid the tracking device."

A stark denial sprang to Angie's lips, but she caught herself. Maybe Detry *had* enlisted Ida to help him. Stranger things had happened. "Her not answering the phone *is* suspicious."

He checked his watch. "By the time we get the vehicles taken care of, it'll be after closing." They were waiting for a friend of

Boone's who owned a glass and body shop to pick up his car to be fixed, and for Boone's rental car to be delivered. "We'll have to wait until tomorrow to check on her."

"Guilty or not, you're worried about her, too."

Boone didn't affirm or deny it. "I'm more worried about keeping you alive right now, to tell you the truth."

"That sounds good to me, too."

"Since we're not going to your mother's until tomorrow, the first thing we have to decide is where you'll stay tonight. My house? It's the safest place I know."

A ritzy lakeside home with every luxury and Boone there, safe? "Staying there is too easy," she vetoed.

"For whoever wants you dead?"

"For us. To get close." She shook her head.

"I'll think of someplace else, then," Boone said, sifting through papers from his desk to put in the briefcase he'd be taking with them to Newton.

His paperwork reminded her of the files she needed. As far as she knew, they wouldn't be returning to his office before they left for Chloe's wedding week. It was time to ask.

"Mind letting me borrow your background investigation on Detry? I'd do the work on my own, but you'd be saving me some time." She braced herself for a refusal.

Boone closed the top of a file folder and unplugged the cord from the back of his laptop. "I'd be making it easier for you to wreck an engagement."

"Or you'd be making it easier for me to save my sister."

He finally shrugged. "You heard a majority of it in court, anyway. I don't see why not. I'll let you read the files when we get where we're going." He slipped his computer into its case and zipped it closed. "Anything else you'd like?"

She grinned. "That's a loaded question. Want to rescind it?"

"I don't like the gleam in your eyes, so maybe I'd better," he said.

An urgent rapping on the front door of the building, which was locked, stopped her from replying.

"Your mechanic?" Angie asked, bending down to palm her weapon.

He shook his head and reached for his gun. "Sonny was just picking up the car, not coming here."

"I hope it's the guy in the Mustang," she whispered. Rising, she followed him through his office doorway into the reception area. "I *really* hope it's the guy in the Mustang."

"Do I need to take your gun away from you?" Boone's eyes never left the front door.

"Hey, Boone," a man's voice yelled out urgently through the door, "it's Sonny Ticker. You got to get out here. I called 911. There's a body in one of the cars next to yours."

Boone signified it was okay with a nod, and Angie holstered her weapon. "That does it," she said. "This day is officially a washout."

"Don't be so negative," Boone said, unlocking and opening the door. "Maybe the car is the Mustang and the body is the shooter, and we won't have to worry about where we'll stay tonight."

She gave him a wide, fake smile. "That would be lovely."

"Of course, the other guy would still be loose. Unless he's out there in the parking garage, too."

"The way this week has been going," she said, "that kind of luck is so not happening." They followed Sonny, a burly, middle-aged man, out the door and down the concrete steps to a walk that led toward the parking garage that Boone owned. "In fact, the way this week's been going, it's probably my car the body is in, and I'm going to get blamed for the guy's murder."

"Uh, hate to interrupt," Sonny said, looking back at them over his shoulder as they passed his tow truck parked on the street in front of the garage, "but it ain't no guy victim. It's a woman."

"You were going to tell us that when?" Boone asked, knowing Sonny wouldn't take offense. The two of them had been friends since Boone had first become a lawyer and driven around in an old truck that was practically taped together, and Sonny had been a mechanic working for someone else.

"You two were busy talking. I don't get paid to interrupt folks."

"Which car?" Angie demanded through gritted teeth.

Sonny pointed.

It was her car. Candy orange. She could see it a mile away. For a second that seemed to linger forever, Angie could not breathe. Her sister. *Please, Lord, no, not her sister.*

She ran to the side of it and peered through the back window, pins and needles in her legs.

It was a woman.

Ida Zlotsky.

"It's not Chloe." Angie turned away from the window, collapsed against the front door of her car, and took deep breaths. Boone could see how pale she was, and how she was shaking again. "There's a dead body in my car," she said. "This should have happened at the cemetery. At least there I would have been expecting it."

"Angel, you're sounding just a bit on the edge," Boone told her.

"Yeah, well, hopefully the next dead body will turn up in your car, and we'll see how you sound."

He slipped his arms around her. Just to hold her up, he told himself.

Yeah, sure.

Interestingly enough, she didn't slip out of his hold, just rested her head against his chest as if he was her support system. In a way, he supposed he was. Maybe he had always been since the moment she'd met him. He liked the idea, but he also knew it wasn't going to last. In a couple of minutes, she would recover from discovering the second dead body within a week, realize she was leaning on the man she couldn't trust and run away again.

While their connection lasted, though, Boone let himself pretend he was her rock and that he deserved to be, just because it felt so good to take care of her.

His gaze drifted to poor Ida.

Who moved.

"She's not dead," he muttered into Angie's soft blond hair. He had to admit he was relieved. He'd really liked Ida.

"Of course she's dead," Angie wailed. "It's that kind of week."

Boone pushed her gently away and pointed to the window. Inside, Ida was rubbing the back of her head and scowling up at them.

"I really thought she was dead," Sonny said from a respectable distance.

"Didn't you check?" Boone asked, pulling open the rear door.

"Why should I? She was dead."

"I'm not dead!" Ida groaned as she took Boone's hand and let him help her out of the car.

"I guess I'd better call 911 back," Sonny said, sounding as if he'd rather not. "Tell them not to come."

"Do that." Boone nodded. "I'll take her to the hospital and have her looked at myself."

Ida frowned. "You will not, and quit talking about me in the third person like I'm dead!"

"You might not be dead, but you sure are grouchy," Sonny said.

"I got hit over the head by a guy in a red Mustang. You'd be grouchy, too." Ida blinked a few more times and took in the shadowy garage and the cars in rented parking places, then she stared back at the car she'd just gotten out of. Finally, her eyes lit on Angie.

"Didn't Handsome say your car was orange? What on earth was I doing in the back of your car?"

Angie moved close to Boone again, even though the initial shock had worn off. "A couple of men in a red Mustang tried to kill us on the interstate this afternoon, Ida. We figure they were after the evidence I dug up."

Ida's mouth went into a big O.

"After they outran the Highway Patrol, they must have gone straight to you," Angie added. "I figure sometime after we got back here, they purposely came here to my car and left you in it as a warning to me." She shivered, realizing the shooters would have been there while she and Boone were just yards away. "But why you, Ida? Do you have some connection to Detry's wife's murder?"

"Of course not!" Ida denied flatly, clearly aghast Angie would say such a thing, her pale green eyes shooting from Angie to Boone and back. "And I have no idea why one of them hit me." She flattened her lips and folded her arms across her chest, staring directly at Angie. After a few seconds, she added, "I have to get back to work."

"You can't go," Angie said.

Ida immediately got a stubborn look on her face that said she absolutely could go, and Angie looked up at Boone and telegraphed him a message with her eyes. Ida couldn't leave, not until they had some information about what the men in the Mustang might have wanted—and why they would have dumped her in Angie's car.

Boone read her concern, or he was thinking the same thing himself.

"Angie just meant it's important you stay with us for a while, Ida. For your own protection," he said, slipping one arm around her shoulders and hugging her.

Angie was impressed. Boone might not know how to comfort women verbally, but he sure did know how to make them feel safe.

"But first," he added, "I want to say we're very happy you're alive."

Ida remained stiff-shouldered and unyielding, but it didn't faze Boone. He just squeezed her again, and finally, Ida gave Boone's shoulder an awkward pat.

"Why do you need me here?" she asked Boone.

"Did you get a good look at the men in the Mustang?"

"Just the one who hit me."

"Then you've just turned into a very important witness in the attempted murder on Angie this afternoon. In fact, the three of us may have to go to the sheriff's department to identify the men and then go to a safe house for at least tonight."

Was that panic she was seeing on Ida's face? Angie opened her mouth to ask the other woman what was scaring her about going to the sheriff's department, when they heard a loud *beep, beep*.

"Too late to call 'em off now—the medics are here!" Sonny yelled from the vehicle entranceway as the paramedics backed their rescue truck inside, red lights flashing.

"Might as well let them look at your head." Boone started to guide Ida to the truck, but she shook off his arm and straightened her shoulders.

"I'll take myself, thank you." She walked away from them, and Angie grabbed Boone.

"Did you see her face when you talked about going to the sheriff's department? She's hiding something."

Boone turned his full attention on Angie. "I think she's just worried about losing her job after leaving the cemetery unattended. I'll talk her into going straight to the house. Maybe Jack can upload some mug shots for us to look through there."

Angie didn't agree with his speculation, but since she was too tired to go back to the sheriff's department, she wasn't going to argue with him. "What's this about a safe house?"

"My house. Ida will enjoy it, I think, and having her there should solve our problem of things being too…easy."

"And we get a chance to get to the bottom of what happened to her. That should work after all."

"Thank you." He grinned down at her.

"Don't get too self-assured. You're so easy to get attached to, Ida might not want to go home."

"How about you?" he asked.

Even she could hear the wistfulness in the sigh that escape her mouth. "There's where Ida and I differ. I don't know that your safe house is going to be that safe for me."

They both knew she wasn't referring to Boone's expensive security system when she talked "safe."

"As for going home, well, you have to know where it is to go there."

Boone took both her hands in his. Any reply he would have made was stopped when Sonny hustled back to them.

"Hey, Boone, you still want me to tow your car in to be fixed, right? Might be easier to hook up to my truck if I move it to the street."

"Sure." Boone let go of Angie's hands to take the car key off his ring and hand it to Sonny. The body shop owner gave them a quick wave of his hand and started for the car. At almost the same time, a new Mercedes, this one white, swung into the garage through the opening and took the first available spot.

"My rental," Boone said. But they both noticed something else at the same time. While they'd been wrapped up in each other, the rescue squad truck had left—and so had Ida.

"Will this day never end?" Angie asked, throwing her palms outward in frustration. "No, wait, I don't want to know."

"I'm ending it right now." Boone went to get his rental car keys from the delivery man. As they walked back to his office, he slipped his cell phone out of his pocket and within seconds, had Jack on the line.

Angie listened to Boone report Ida's earlier kidnapping and her current disappearance, and then ask Jack if Angie could spend the night with him and his wife, Missy. He nodded their assent at Angie almost immediately, which set her mind at ease.

Emotionally, she was vulnerable to Boone, and she didn't want to spend time at his home, let alone overnight. She'd married her first husband out of lust she mistook for love, and that had been a disaster. Better to follow what God wanted, which was total propriety when it came to unmarried people, and not put herself in a vulnerable place.

Obviously, she still loved Boone somewhere in her heart, or she wouldn't be hurting so much inside or even entertaining thoughts of going to his house. She knew the man better than to think he would change. She was just falling back to her dream of finding love and starting a family, and she had to stop and focus on God again.

Boone was still talking to Jack when they reached his office, which he unlocked and entered, and locked again behind them. Something beyond Ida's escapades was happening, she could tell by the way Boone's eyes crinkled at the edges, and by his crisp, quick answers. Finally, just when she didn't think she could handle the suspense any longer, he pocketed his phone.

"There's news."

"Spill it, Boone."

"On the Colt you dug up, Detry's prints were found, but so were two more on the grip that aren't his wife's and that didn't come back as a match to anyone in the database. Jack's got DNA testing in the works, but he was told there might not be enough usable blood evidence on the gun for that due to the way it was stored. The unmatched prints will be run on the national database, so the results are pending and we can't mention anything to anyone, including your sister." He probed her eyes. "You know what those extra prints mean, don't you?"

"Yeah. They mean Detry or his wife could have shown off the Colt to one of their friends at some time."

His mouth tightened. "It's also possible someone left those prints when they murdered Laurie Detry," he said. "Someone Cliff knew, which was why he covered up for him. If that person thinks Cliff told you his identity, that could well be why those men were using your head for target practice this afternoon."

She went stormily silent. Boone felt the sides being drawn up by her, almost as though this were a court case. She was mistakenly trying to prove Warren Detry murdered his wife, for her sister's sake. Boone was still claiming Detry's innocence. Only now he planned to play the case differently. He would try to figure out who *was* guilty of Laurie Detry's murder to keep Angie alive. This time around, he wasn't for Detry, he was for Angie.

And somehow, he'd show her that. The only type of love he had to give her was to protect her—that was all he really knew how to do for anyone. Then, at the end when she was safe from outside forces, he would walk away from her because he couldn't be what she wanted. But right now, all that mattered was keeping her alive and repaying the wrong he'd done her.

He'd promised her that.

FIVE

Upon waking up in Jack and Missy's guest room the next morning, Angie was at a loss as to her next step. She still had no proof for her sister. Detry's prints on the murder weapon were inconclusive. That men were trying to kill her was good, but she couldn't tie them to Detry yet. She couldn't even identify them, despite two hours of mugshot-gazing the night before with Boone. She wondered if Cliff was still the answer. If he had squirreled away one piece of evidence, he might have others, too.

The solution came to her suddenly, as she was dressing in fresh jeans and a zip-front shirt with short sleeves that happened to be the same shade as Boone's eyes. Go figure. Cliff's desk might hold a clue, if it hadn't been cleared out yet for his replacement. It was worth a try. Maybe he'd left notes about the case there or a list of people to question, or something.

Boone wouldn't appreciate her need to search Cliff's desk, of course. He wouldn't see it as ethical. But Cliff had wanted to put everything right again—he'd as much as said that in his phone message—and if she found proof Detry was guilty, she could bring about justice for Cliff, and save her sister. Her conscience was clear.

Evading Boone wasn't a problem—he wasn't there. Jack had left her a note on the breakfast counter in front of a bag of fresh bagels and a half-full coffeemaker.

Missy went to work, I've been called into work for damage control and Boone's coming at ten. He says not to go anywhere.

Dear, sweet Boone. Even if they knew where she was now, she doubted the Mustang guys would follow her into a police station. Flipping the note over, she wrote where she'd be so he wouldn't worry, and then called a cab. Less than a half-hour later, at the police station, she paid the driver and hurried inside through the special entrance reserved for officers. She wouldn't need a ride home. She had a feeling Boone would be waiting for her when she exited.

The first place she headed was to the lockers. Even if she had no success finding anything helpful at Cliff's desk, she wanted to get the fresh uniform she kept in her locker as a spare if hers got soiled or ripped while on duty to wear to Cliff's funeral that afternoon. Coming out of the station with it would also help Boone calm down.

The locker rooms and police lounge were down a set of stairs in the basement. In the women's locker room, a small closet compared to the men's, she opened hers and pulled out the opaque garment bag she kept her extra uniform in. Almost as an afterthought, she got her bulletproof vest, as well. The way things were going, she figured it might come in handy. Zipping up the bag, she headed into the stairwell. Two flights of stairs later, she was in the second-floor hallway, peeking into the detective squad room.

The only person in there was Della, an efficient and no-nonsense civilian in her thirties who was really good at her job of answering the phones and keeping the public in line when they came up to see a detective. Rumor had it she didn't much care for Chief Gregg, whose office was to the far side of the room. Angie was counting on that now.

Della peered up over her glasses at Angie with a displeased look. "You're not supposed to be here," she said in a singsong voice.

"I need a favor," Angie said. "It's about Cliff's death, and the chief wouldn't like it if he caught me."

The words *"chief wouldn't like it"* seemed to unlock a door. Della smiled.

"I want to—"

"Wait." She held up her hand. "I don't want to know. I need to run the chief's memo down to the front desk and get a soda. You're on your own if you get caught. I need my job."

"Thanks."

"The chief took a couple of folders from Cliff's desk, but otherwise, anything personal should still be there." Della picked up a piece of paper, rounded the desk and stopped in front of her. "I'm sorry for your loss. Cliff thought of you as a daughter." Then she was gone.

A lump rose in Angie's throat, but she swallowed and strode to Cliff's desk. A quick scan of the two papers on top told her they were unimportant office memos issued a couple days before his death. Cliff's angular printing was on the side of one. "Victory Church, 7:00 p.m., men's Bible study. Starts Friday night."

He'd planned to attend Bible study the night he committed suicide? That didn't make sense.

Bending, she opened his personal file cabinet and pulled out the folder marked "Expense Receipts." He'd told her if she ever made detective to label a file by that name and keep anything she didn't want anyone else to snoop into in it, because no one wanted someone else's expense receipts, especially not the people you worked for.

Boy, she missed him.

She slipped a large rubber band from Cliff's collection around the file and slid it into her garment bag, her senses on full alert for any voices. She went to the squad file cabinet and quickly found the Detry murder file. Less than a year old, it hadn't been archived yet. As a responding officer, she had a right to read it, she just couldn't take it off of the premises. So she copied Cliff's typed report, reading snatches as the pages came through, and then put the copy in her bag. Walking to the file cabinet, she was about to replace the folder when a voice barked at her from the doorway.

"What are you doing?"

Detective Joe Santiago. According to Cliff, the slim man with wavy, dark brown hair was all attitude and trouble. Sneaky, too. She had no idea how long he'd been watching her, so she told the truth.

"I was consulting a file. Now I'm putting it back."

Santiago scowled and covered the distance between them in seconds. He grabbed the file and checked the label.

"You trying to cause more problems about the Detry case? Not wise."

Oh, now she was getting irritated. "Are you threatening me?"

"I hope not," Della said from the door. "What's going on, Detective Santiago?"

"Where were you?" Santiago asked as the receptionist joined them, waving the file at her.

Della's eyebrow lifted. "Doing my job." She took the file, jerked open the cabinet, filed it and shoved the drawer closed. "Officer Delitano, are you supposed to be working today?"

"No." Angie started to leave, but Santiago caught her arm.

"I saw you put something in the bag," he said.

Della let out a huge sigh, took the garment bag from Angie, and turned it until the front was facing her, away from Santiago. Unzipping it, she frowned.

"You know the rules. Nothing leaves the office without permission." Pulling out only the pages Angie had just copied, Della handed them to Santiago, shook her head at Angie disappointedly, and zipped the bag closed, leaving Cliff's file folder inside.

There was no way she could have missed it. "I'm sorry, Officer. I'll have to write this up. You'd better go now."

Angie sent a pointed look at Santiago, who let go of her arm. In less than four seconds, she was out of there. She wasted no time flying down the steps and had almost made it outside when she ran right into Jack Callahan—and Police Chief Roy Gregg.

Glory. She should probably start the whole week over, because it wasn't getting any better.

Jack looked up first and rolled his eyes when he saw her. Oh, she was in trouble. He didn't say a word, but she figured the chief would have no such self-control.

"Speaking of Officer Delitano," Gregg said to Jack, "here she is." His piercing gaze changed direction to her. "What are you doing here? You're supposed to be on compassionate leave."

Gregg, a muscular man in his fifties, with a military-short haircut, prided himself on being a ladies' man, and kept in good shape. He also prided himself on running a tight department. She, he had pointed out after the Detry trial, was his one black mark. He didn't want another, and she could see that thought reflected in his eyes now. He'd look for a reason to fire her.

Like she was going to make it that easy.

"I stopped by to get my other uniform out of my locker for Cliff's funeral this afternoon." She hoisted up the garment bag an inch or so and let him fill in any blanks so she wouldn't have to lie. They already knew what had happened to her other uniform—it was stained with Cliff's blood from when she had tried to revive him.

Gregg glanced at the garment bag. "He didn't die in the line of duty. The uniform isn't required."

"I'm honoring him by wearing it." Her eyes flared up, and she dared him to disagree.

He stared at her. Since she didn't feel guilty, she didn't flinch. Finally, he nodded. "Fine. You should know, then, the funeral's been canceled until further notice."

"What? Why?" she asked, stunned.

"Can't say. Just make yourself available to Chief Deputy Callahan here if he wants to question you about finding Haggis. He's from the sheriff's department." Turning, he walked away from them toward the stairwell.

"That man needs to do some shopping at the 'lighten up' store," Jack muttered, slipping his hand under her elbow and propelling her toward the exit. "I wonder what made him that way."

She glanced sideways at Jack. He was a year younger than Boone at thirty-two, had short, black hair and a broad-shouldered build like Boone, but his eyes were black, and he was a couple of inches shorter and even more fond of a quick comeback. According to Boone, his friend was also insatiably curious about people and how they ticked. Unfortunately, Angie was in no mood to delve into Gregg's mind. She agreed with Jack's assessment, but she had bigger problems than her boss.

"What's going on, Jack?" she asked. "Why was the funeral delayed?"

Jack leaned forward and pushed open the door for her. "I'm only going to tell you because your life could be in danger. You need to keep it quiet. We don't want anyone fleeing to avoid prosecution because the news leaked."

"I'm a cop, Jack. I can keep my mouth shut."

He didn't take offense. "Which way?" he asked, indicating the quiet parking lot.

"Wherever Boone is parked," she said sweetly.

"You left the house without him knowing, and you think he's not going to wash his hands of you?"

"He won't. I'm too much of a challenge for him," she replied.

Sure enough, she could see Boone walking across the parking lot, headed right toward them.

"He's got it bad," Jack said, spotting him, too. "I'd better tell you about Cliff before he gets here and I can't get a word in edgewise." He lowered his voice. "Since he was involved in the hiding of evidence in a felony and then showed up dead unexpectedly, the sheriff wants his death investigated, in case it's murder. The body won't be released for burial until they're sure one way or the other."

He paused, and gave her the sternest no nonsense look he could. "That's another reason you need to listen to Boone when he tells you to stay put, Angie. Cliff might have taken a wrong turn, but by reputation, he was an excellent cop as far as instincts and reflexes. If it was murder, apparently he never saw the shot coming. If he could get taken totally by surprise, so could you."

The horror of poor Cliff looking up to see a gun in his face sent fresh grief washing over her, but she had to remain strong. She had too much to do.

"Who outside the department knows about the investigation?" she asked.

"Just you, Boone and now Chief Gregg. That's why I was here, to inform him."

Boone reached them. "You're riding back with me," he said.

"That ought to give *fun* a whole new definition," Angie said. Boone didn't smile. Uh-oh. She and Jack fell into step beside Boone, with Jack stopping when he got to his sheriff's department cruiser.

"I'll meet you back at the house," he said.

She waved her fingers at him.

"What are you doing here?" Boone demanded.

"You want the answer that will calm you down, or the truth?"

"Your choice, Angie. Just make it good." His eyes started scanning the lot again as he went right into his bodyguard mode.

"I came to get my uniform for Cliff's funeral. What a wasted trip, huh?"

Boone's mouth remained straight. "So what's the answer that will calm me down?"

He didn't sound like he was kidding, so she didn't joke. "I wanted to see if Cliff had any notes on his desk that might explain why he came clean, who else might have been involved, etc."

"Did you find out anything?" he asked, reaching out to open the passenger-side door for her. She got in and pulled it shut herself. He was already rounding the car.

Fortunately, she had seen some information she could quote to him. What she wasn't going to do was tell him she had Cliff's file. She would give it to Jack, but only after she'd read it. In Cliff's notes could be something that pointed directly to Detry as his wife's killer—and her only chance to save her sister's life.

"Cliff's investigation on Laurie Detry's background seemed thorough." She watched Boone start up the car and put it in gear. "She coordinated a yearly Christmas toy drive for the Copper City Police Department and had a clean record, no hint of affairs, not even a parking ticket." She took a breath. "That's all I had a chance to read." From the case file, anyway.

They were back in Jack's neighborhood before Boone replied. "First, let me say I know you're not telling me everything. So don't think you're getting away with anything."

"It's nice to know I'm evenly matched."

"I'm not even going to shake my head at that. Ida Zlotsky's gone into hiding."

"Whoa. Jack's men found this out?" she guessed.

Boone nodded. "One of them ran by the cemetery this morning to see if he could take her statement about how she ended up in your vehicle. She wasn't there. According to the cemetery's owner, she quit last night. He's angry enough to put her in one of the graves himself."

"Over an employee quitting?"

"There's more to it than that. The surveillance cameras we saw at the cemetery do work. They feed into the office computer. Part of Ida's job was to back up the surveillance onto disks."

"Ida lied," Angie breathed. Then she rapped her left hand against the side of her head. "What is this world coming to? And why did I actually believe her?"

"You should be more cynical, Angie."

"I will now. So why did she lie to us, do you figure?"

"I'm not sure. The most recent surveillance backups for this month were missing from the safe, and the hard drive was wiped clean with one of those security shredders. Maybe she was protecting someone."

Angie remembered Ida's rapid breathing and her wide eyes after her kidnapping. "We really need to talk to her."

"Us and Jack," Boone said, pulling into Jack's driveway. "Unfortunately, she's not at the address her employer gave Jack's deputy. Her landlady is as upset as the cemetery owner. She told the deputy Ida wouldn't give a forwarding address. That it was life or death she hide."

Angie's mouth went into a circle of surprise as she undid her seat belt. "Her exact words—'life or death'?"

Boone nodded. "In her apartment, the deputy found what they think are the missing disks of the cemetery footage, dated through last Thursday."

So Ida must still have the footage from Friday till yesterday. Angie leaned back in her seat as they waited for Jack to pull up and let them inside. Cliff had died on Friday. Was it related? What was on that footage? Had the men in the Mustang been looking for it when they took Ida?

"At least we know she wasn't kidnapped again." That was comforting. "Something could be on those disks related to those men in the Mustang that's really important." Maybe they'd picked up Detry and there was a shot of them together. "We really need to find her and that missing disk." She looked at Boone. "Right?"

"Wrong. We're supposed to leave for your mother's house this afternoon," he reminded her.

"That can be postponed." Especially if a chance existed she could get concrete evidence to convince her sister to stop the wedding.

Boone's eyes were saying no. "I think we should go today. You'll be safer if you aren't in the city."

"Safer by being around the man who hired two men to kill me? I don't think so."

Jack was pulling up behind them, so Boone and Angie got out. She rounded the car to Boone's side, bringing the garment bag she'd kept in her arms the whole ride. Boone frowned down at it, then turned his attention back to their topic.

"Just to show you I'm trying, I'll stretch my imagination and assume Detry did hire them," he said. "He's not going to do anything that would get in the way of getting what he wants, which is keeping your sister happy long enough to marry her. I think that kind of eliminates killing you in front of Chloe."

She couldn't argue that. Jack approached them as Boone added, "On the other hand…" She'd known that was coming. Boone was, after all, a lawyer.

"If someone else murdered Laurie Detry, then he might want you dead because he either really wants the evidence he thinks you still have, or he wants you out of commission, thinking Cliff might have told you enough before he died to hang him. Whoever it is apparently has money at his disposal—enough to get tracking devices for my car and, according to Jack, yours, and hire hit men. We'll basically be hiding in Newton. We need to go soon, Angel."

She couldn't stand it when he called her that. The gentle memories of when everything was good between them that came flooding back were so hard to bear. She wanted to run from them. From him.

Jack left them to walk ahead and unlock his front door. Angie watched him as she thought about her answer to Boone.

"If you're right about this guy being unknown, going to Newton means I might be bringing the danger to Chloe and my mother."

"I'll be your extra set of eyes on the way there, remember? Together, we can make sure we're not followed." Boone's expression told her he was not giving up on leaving today. She pursed her lips at him, meeting him stubborn for stubborn.

She was good at that.

"Hey, you two, remember me?" Jack waved his hand in the air and opened the door to get them moving inside. "Here's my opinion on you two leaving—it's a good idea. You'll be safer if you get out of Copper City and give us a little time to catch this guy." He took off his suit jacket, threw it on the sofa and headed toward the kitchen. Angie ran up the stairs, hung up her uniform and hid the file, then joined Jack and Boone.

They'd already filled their coffee mugs and were sitting at the table. Jack pointed to the bag on the counter. "So how about it, Angie?"

"I'd love a bagel," she told them, purposely ignoring his true question, which was if she would leave for Newton peacefully, or if she wanted to be browbeaten. She dug into the bag for a whole-wheat one, cut and toasted it. They were still waiting for her real answer by the time she slathered it with cream cheese and brought her meal to the table.

She sighed. "Isn't it more logical to use me as bait to lure the murderer out of hiding?"

Jack and Boone exchanged a quick, serious look. They were keeping something from her, she suddenly realized. Well, that was okay—she was doing the same thing with Cliff's file.

She still wasn't caving to them. She knew Boone liked to be in control, and he wasn't always right. Not only that, she was in no hurry to return to the house where she'd grown up in Newton, not without proof to help her plead her case to Chloe.

And there were the memories, too, that she didn't want to deal with, but she shoved those aside.

"You need to go," Boone told her. "You don't want to miss this chance to reunite with your family."

"Boone—" It was like he was ignoring reality.

Jack put down his coffee. "You can't do anything here, Angie. We have Ida's license-plate number and the make and model of her vehicle. We'll be looking for her, but chances are she's not even in the area."

Even though he wasn't saying a thing, she was well aware of Boone's penetrating blue eyes watching her, waiting for her to give in.

Jack was doing the dirty work, it seemed. "You'll be in danger if you stay here. Someone was keeping track of you, Angie. We had your car swept this morning and found another tracking device."

"Boy, I missed a lot when I slept in, didn't I?" she asked.

Jack didn't budge. "Whoever added the other device to Boone's Mercedes knows you're close enough to Boone that you would go to him, and he would help you. When you took off together and ended up at the cemetery, that someone probably sent the guys in the Mustang to get the evidence and/or kill you. When they didn't succeed, they went back to see if you'd told

Ida anything. Maybe they knew about the surveillance disks, maybe they didn't. We don't know how they fit in yet.

"We're speculating they decided to leave you some sort of message not to talk by dumping poor Ida in your car. Why they didn't kill her we don't know, unless it's because she really doesn't know anything important."

"Yeah. It's just me they want dead." Her bagel forgotten, Angie moved her jaw back and forth. It was finally getting to her. "I should be glad they didn't rig my apartment to explode when we went back to get my clothes last night."

"I thought of that," Boone told her. "That's why I walked inside first."

"I love that quality in a man," she said. She couldn't help it—she started softening toward him again. It must have shown on her face, because he smiled at her.

Jack got up and poured the rest of his coffee down the drain. "We're getting nowhere with this discussion. No offense, Angie, but right now, I need to be looking for this jerk who wants you dead. I don't have time to babysit you and Boone. The two of you really need to go to Newton."

Jack knew he didn't have to babysit them. Angie had a feeling he was just backing up Boone, who was behind this push to get her to the wedding. Again, why? Why, when they could catch the murderer within a couple of days just by letting on that she had evidence, and luring him into a trap?

"Boone, you and I need to have a discussion—alone. Maybe in the living room."

"Great idea," Jack said, a little too eagerly for her. "I'm going to the office. You'll have all the privacy in the world. Talk." With a wave, he retrieved his suit jacket and left out the door leading to the garage.

Grabbing his coffee mug, Boone walked out into the living

room and sank onto the Callahans' plush blue velvet sofa. Angie grabbed her coffee, walked to the armchair that matched the sofa and sat, her fingertips sinking into the soft upholstery.

Boone was waiting for her to say yes, she was going into hiding. He wasn't going to like her answer. But she was going to give it.

SIX

"I'm glad Jack told me there's a possibility Cliff did not commit suicide," she said, sadness still lacing her voice over her mentor's death. "I'm thankful I didn't miss the signs he was so depressed he was willing to take his own life." She gave her head a shake, and Boone watched her pale blond waves dance. "On the other hand, I just realized that had I been a few minutes earlier in getting to his house, I might have been killed, too."

Boone hadn't thought of that. He could have turned on the local news Saturday morning and discovered the one woman who'd ever given him hope for a happy future had been brutally gunned down. His gut clenched.

"That's why you need me to stick by you," he said.

She leaned forward to get his attention. "I'm going to tell you what I should have said to Ida—I truly believe God is watching over me. I'm depending on Him, not man. Cliff's death and the bullet missing my head showed me that."

She was totally discounting luck and the fact that he had kept her from rising up seconds before the shot cracked through the car—and giving all the credit to God. Boone would have pointed that out, but he was unsure he wanted to get into an argument over God when there was something more important to talk about: their future together.

So he would let her get this out of her system.

"You really think there is someone in control up there even when the most awful things happen?"

She nodded. "I have to believe God is in control. Everything happens for a purpose."

"Even my father being dragged off to prison for something he didn't do, changing his life forever?" Where had that come from? Even Angie looked taken aback.

She recovered well, though. In seconds, her dark green eyes were once again serene. "Yes, even that. Look how it affected your life. You decided nothing was going to stop you from helping others in his position. That was God working."

"No, that was me taking control of my life and my decisions."

"You wouldn't have succeeded unless you were going down the road God wanted you to be on." She hesitated. "Look at me. Every time I've tried to be in control of my own life, I've made a wrong decision that's made me miserable."

"Like…" He let the words drift off. He wanted to say like he had, in court, the day he'd lost her. But they'd had problems even before that fateful court day. She might bring that up, and he didn't want to get into it—yet.

She took his "like" as a question. "Like the wrong decision that led to my getting kicked out of my house." Not wanting him to think less of her, Angie had never explained what she had done to make her mother and sister change from apathetic to hating her. She really didn't want to tell him now, but it was more important that he see the point she wanted to make to him—he should not try to control her life, because God was already in charge.

"When I was growing up, Dad had been the only one who ever paid any attention to me, but he was a long-distance trucker and gone for weeks at a stretch. Then he died."

She stopped speaking, remembering how horrified she had been when she'd heard that the only person she'd ever sensed real love from wasn't coming home again. Her world had collapsed, and she had cried for two days. Even her mother had been worried. For the first time, she'd been almost kind, bringing her meals in her room and not insisting she go back to school.

But crying hadn't brought her father back, so she'd dried her tears and gotten on with life. Her mother had resumed ignoring her, and her sister had paid attention to her only if she wanted something. For the next seven years, she'd felt like an undiscovered planet at the cold, dark end of the universe.

"Angie?"

"Dad died," she repeated. "I was ten. I don't know why Mom treated me like I wasn't there, but she did. She wasn't abusive or anything like that, but whenever Chloe came home from school, her eyes lit up. When she looked at me, it was like she was looking at a stranger. There weren't any questions about my day, any real interest in my life."

Boone sat up straight. He didn't want to interrupt her, but he had to. "Is that why you don't want children, Angie?"

She nodded solemnly. "I'm afraid I'll be the same type of mother—especially since I never had a good example of one. And I can't help but think I'm a lot like her. I take a long time to grow close to people. I'm not really the nurturing type. She never was, either, not even with Chloe. I don't want to have a baby and find out, too late, that it's some basic personality lack or trait that makes us that way and I'll make my child miserable."

Boone didn't know what to say. He knew some people weren't meant to be parents. He didn't think Angie was one, but how to tell her that? He was clueless.

Angie took a deep breath. This was so difficult, getting into a major problem in their relationship she was nowhere near ready to discuss. And remembering how alone she'd felt. But she had to go on. Boone needed to know why she didn't want him pushing her to return.

"I guess I took out feeling unloved on Chloe. She's three years older than I am, but when I was almost eighteen, she was still living at home, working as a teller in a bank, going to church and being the perfect daughter. She started dating a young bank officer at work, and pretty soon, they were engaged."

She blinked a couple times and tried to rub the tension out of her jaw. She had to get this out for Boone's sake.

"Her fiancé, Tony, started flirting with me when Chloe left the room. Pretty soon, he was telling me he didn't know how on earth he'd ended up engaged to Chloe, but he didn't want to marry her. She wasn't the free spirit he'd thought she was."

"She wouldn't go to bed with him."

She nodded. "She was a Christian. I thought she was playing holier-than-thou. I didn't understand back then, Boone, and I made mistakes."

"You were only seventeen," Boone said, as though he totally understood.

And desperate for love. "Tony broke off their engagement without telling her why, and we dated each other in secret. A neighbor saw him pick me up and asked Chloe about it, and Chloe started yelling that I had stolen her fiancé, and Mom kicked me out on my eighteenth birthday, saying she'd done her duty and enough was enough." She raised her eyes to him again, blinking back her tears. "I shouldn't have done it, but I was so desperate for someone to care, and Tony did."

Boone rose to his feet and held out his arms, and so help her, as stupid as it was, she flew into his arms and rested her head against his shoulder.

"I understand, Angel. It's okay."

"I wasn't saved then. If I was, I would have let God guide me like He was guiding Chloe."

Once again he was silent, and for a minute, she cried, wetting his shirt with her tears of regret and pain. When she realized that, she pulled back and reached for a tissue from the side table.

"I'm sorry," she said, trying to mop him up.

"There's some dry shirt left if you need to keep crying."

She tried to resist smiling, but the corners of her mouth twitched. Boone could always make her laugh, even when she was miserable. How did he do that?

"That's better." He took her arm and guided her over to sit on the couch by him. "Go ahead. Tell me the rest."

"You know the rest. Tony died in a shoot-out with the police."

"You never gave me the details."

That was true. She'd shied away from telling him her past, afraid the successful, important man who lived for the law would think less of her and drop her. Now that she knew they didn't have a future, it didn't matter if he knew.

"Tony lived for the thrill. I lived for Tony. We got married right away. He found a position at a different bank so he wouldn't have to work around Chloe. I graduated high school, went to work in a supermarket and started taking college courses at night. We were happy for over two years, until Tony lost his job. He said his boss had it in for him. He couldn't get another job in Newton, so we moved to Copper City, where he said he had friends." She gave a heartless chuckle. "They got work for him. Yeah, sure, selling drugs. I stumbled upon some while he was home and confronted him. He told me he'd been laid off, and it was only temporary to get some money for us, and then he would never do it again. The second he left the house that night, I called it in. The officer I talked to—I never did write down his name—took his information, and told me they would investigate, and I sat back and waited. But no one came to talk to me."

Boone frowned. "Did you find out why?"

She shook her head. "Cliff said later, maybe it was because I admitted Tony had taken the drugs with him, and it would have been a he said/she said situation. To this day, I don't know. After a week of thinking they would arrest him, I started making plans to move out and divorce him. I needed to save some money first, since I didn't have enough for a new place. But then he died."

"What happened?" Boone slipped his arm around her shoulders. She leaned back, grateful for the contact while she finished the story.

"From what Cliff told me much later, one of the detectives found out his son was buying from Tony and got a warrant to arrest. Apparently Tony got tipped off they were coming minutes before—no one knows by who. He got into his car and took off. I was the one who woke up to the police busting down the door."

"Oh, sweetheart." His fingers caressed the back of her hair, and she leaned into them.

"I told them the make and model number of Tony's car. They chased him and when he got out, he was waving the gun, saying the cops were going to kill him, and he wasn't going down without a fight. I never understood that, but maybe he'd started taking drugs and was delusional. I have no idea. He fired the weapon and they had no choice but to shoot him. The last words he uttered were 'Angie doesn't know.'"

"Know what?"

She lifted her shoulders in question. She was almost done. It felt good to finally be telling Boone all this, clearing the air between them. He needed to understand her heart, why it was so difficult for her to return to Newton like the prodigal daughter and why all her decisions had to be God-driven ones.

"I was so angry with Tony for doing this to me—ruining the

perfect life that I'd set up and taking away my happiness. For not putting me first in his life. And I was sad, too. I was right back where I started before my marriage—totally alone. I started throwing Tony's things out the window the second the officers left my apartment. A heart-shaped pillow I gave him on Valentine's Day bopped Cliff on his head."

A throaty laugh escaped from Boone.

"I know. Fortunately, it was Cliff. He turned right around and came up to have a talk with me. It all poured out, everything about my life, including how furious I was at Tony for failing me. Cliff asked me if I wanted to come to church with him and his wife. He told me that human beings were imperfect, and we should never look to them to keep us going, but that God wouldn't fail us."

She swiveled until she was facing him. "My whole point in telling you this is that I can't live for a man again. That ended in disaster. That's why you and I had problems. When I met you, I lost focus on God, putting all my faith in you. So much I was starting to change my life for you."

"So you're saying you can only have a future with someone who is a believer."

She winced. "I'm saying I have to follow God's lead, not yours, whether it's considering a future together or going to Newton."

"And if He leads you right into danger, or keeps you from doing something that would bring you happiness?"

"Then He does, because God knows best. That's where faith comes in." She knew she wasn't explaining that as well as she could, and that was her fault. She needed to study more, take some courses in how to explain why all of this was so important—something.

"How do you know if you're doing what God wants, or what you want?"

How *did* she know? "I pray first, read the Bible or talk to another person who is strong in the faith. Usually the right thing to do will become absolutely clear to me."

"And if it doesn't?"

"Then I wait. I don't try to take control myself. I see my old self in you, Boone. If you're not in control of every detail of your life so you can avoid pain, you aren't happy."

His gaze was unflinching. "I don't look at this the same way as you. I don't want to leave everything in my life to chance, or to some God that might not even exist. I have to go after what I want, cover all angles. The only one I can depend on is myself. I found that out early on."

"That's because you're angry with God. If you would just turn to Him, He'll soften your heart."

"If that was true, if God softened your heart, wouldn't you be more eager to talk to your mother and try to straighten things out?"

"I do want to straighten things out. But right now, it's complicated. I have to put Chloe first. If I say the wrong thing to Mom, Chloe will be furious, and I'll have no hope of reaching her about Detry."

"You're scared."

"And you're pushing. Why?" She gazed at the handsome face of the man she'd once thought she would marry. Could Boone just be using her faith to manipulate her into doing what he wanted?

He wasn't answering her.

"I really want to know, Boone. You can keep me safe here if we plotted a trap for the shooters."

"What if I fail?" Boone asked. "I don't want to see you wind up like Cliff. Or do you think that's what your God wants, in order to teach me some sort of lesson?"

"That's not how God is, Boone." A shudder went through her at the thought. "But I don't think being worried about failing me is why you're doing this."

"You wound me."

"Not yet," she said. "But I could consider it. I think you want me to talk to my mother in the hopes that will fix everything, I'll want children and we'll get back together. But that won't happen. You'll still want career first, and family second, and if God gets in your way, you'll manipulate things until He's not. And that's not what I want."

Boone leveled his gaze on her. She wanted him to trust God. To have faith. But her faith had nothing to do with why she had walked away after the trial without trying to work things out between them. That was more like lack of faith, if he was understanding her. Leaving was how she handled big problems in her life. She cared so much about having a family, but she was afraid of her emotions and being hurt, so she ran. She needed to realize she had to start dealing with her past so she could have a bright future.

A future that probably wouldn't be with him. He could put her first, but he couldn't put a God he didn't understand first. Her faith would always be between them, no matter how much he wanted her in his life.

But he did want her to be happy, and he didn't think that was going to happen until someone stepped in, because if she realized it or not, she was fighting her God about going to fix her life in Newton. It wasn't manipulation, it was love.

Don't go there, he warned himself.

"I want you in Newton because you won't try to build a relationship with your mother unless there's something forcing you into it. In fact, I think you'd do anything to avoid them possibly hurting you again—including walking into extreme danger."

"That's crazy." She shook her head until her blond waves flapped against her cheeks. "Nobody would choose facing a murderer instead of facing their mother and sister."

"You just said you would, if God was leading you to it."

She avoided his eyes, so he tilted her chin up with his finger and made her face him. "You say I should let God be in control of my life. So is refusing to reconcile with your family Him in control—or is it you? Because, Angel, right now it seems like one of those decisions you're going to end up regretting, and that would mean it's you, not God, making it."

He took a deep breath. "You want me to understand about turning my life over to God? It would help if you would do it yourself."

Angie watched him walk out of the room. No, no, no. Self-examination was not on her agenda. On the other hand, serving God was, and to do that, she had to at least consider what Boone was pointing out to her.

Was she hoping that she would get the proof she needed here against Detry so she would never have to go back and face her mother? Or was she merely being extremely cautious, needing to get concrete evidence for Chloe before she ventured back to Newton and went up against the man who maybe wanted her dead? At least she really believed it was him.

If she went to Newton, would she be doing what God wanted, or allowing Boone to manipulate her again?

Here in Copper City, she would also be in direct danger, especially if she tried to lure the Mustang shooters out into the open. But then she might get the evidence she needed to get Chloe to call off the wedding, if the shooters confessed Detry hired them. And she would not have to go through the pain of facing her mother.

She frowned at how happy she would be about that. Score one more for Boone.

In Newton, the danger would be lessened, if only because Detry probably would not try to have her killed right there by her sister. But with no evidence going in, convincing her sister about Detry would be very difficult. And she would have to face her mother. The idea of that made her very nervous, yes. But Boone would see that she was trying to live her faith.

Was she rebelling against God by wanting to stay in Copper City? Was her real problem that and hard-heartedness toward her mother? That was the jaw-dropper. It might be. And while she was in Newton, would she be accomplishing other purposes for Him? Like helping to get Boone to see that even though she stumbled all the time, she was trying desperately to live as God wanted her to?

She knew what the answers were, but she didn't want to accept them. Not yet. There was Cliff's file to go through. Maybe that held the proof she needed to get Detry for something and save her sister without her setting foot in Newton—or facing her past.

She ran up the stairs, shut the door to the guest room, and got the file out. There were some expense receipts, unclaimed. Her mouth twisted in amusement, despite her worry. Receipts in the receipt file? Cliff must have been reforming his ways all around.

There were a few larger invoices, handwritten, with some sort of code on them she didn't bother to decipher. She was looking for notes. There weren't any, just the receipts. She'd give the file to Boone for Jack.

She took a deep breath. Once again, God had made what He wanted clear. First, she needed to apologize to Him for rebelling and make an effort to soften up her heart where her mother was concerned. Then she had to apologize to Boone and tell him her decision.

Being a Christian was not for wimps.

SEVEN

By five that afternoon, Angie and Boone were getting out of Boone's rented Mercedes in front of her mother's two-car garage in the working-class neighborhood where she'd grown up, about an hour west of Copper City, near Cincinnati.

Two cars were already parked inside the garage, and a brand-new Lexus was on the other side of them in the driveway. Chloe knew she and Boone were coming, so she must have invited Detry. Great. She might as well get the initial contact over with.

As Boone hoisted their suitcases out of the trunk of his Mercedes, she examined her childhood home. It was three stories high, counting the attic, and for some odd reason seemed much larger than when she'd been seventeen and eager to find a way out of all that sadness. Back then the house felt like a small prison she couldn't escape.

She turned back to Boone. He read her eyes and said, "Don't worry, Angie. It's not the same as before. I'm here."

His reassurance sent bittersweet emotions through her. She was glad Boone was with her, and that he hadn't been that angry about the file, which he'd given to Jack. He had been right to lay out his case to get her to come. She hoped he was really thinking about God, and not using her belief in God to manipulate her. She couldn't imagine he would do that, but then, she had never thought he would betray her like he had, either.

"You ready?" He had a suitcase in each hand, waiting for her to lead the way.

She started walking, heard the front door open and raised her head. Filing out onto the wide wooden porch were her mother and Chloe. Warren came out last and slipped his arm around Chloe's waist.

As she looked into his soulless stare, fear gutted her and she stopped dead. Her legs turned to lead and she couldn't resume her steps. Time stood still. For a few seconds she couldn't take a full breath.

Detry was not going to try anything this week. The logic behind Boone's earlier statement was valid. At this time, her real problem was not Detry, but not wanting to face two people who hadn't seemed to care if she lived or died. Chloe seemed to have changed, but if her mother hadn't, she'd be devastated. That she had wronged Chloe made it even harder.

That's what she told herself. It wasn't Detry frightening her. He had no power over her. Only the past did.

"I'm still here, Angel," Boone said in her ear.

She met his eyes and drew strength from him. Boone cared. She had to remember that, no matter how badly he infuriated her with his controlling ways. Blinking several times, she forced herself to meet Detry's eyes again.

This time, they looked normal. With his styled hair and a dark blue suit that looked every bit as expensive as one of Boone's, he resembled more the successful account executive Chloe said he was now than the monster she thought him to be.

She gave him a stiff, reluctant nod. He barely smiled, and a chill ran through her.

Chloe slipped out from Detry's arm and rushed down the porch steps to meet her halfway, throwing her arms around her and hugging her tightly. "I'm so glad you came. I wasn't really sure you would."

Hurts from the past throbbed anew, but facing the smiling woman in front of her, whose eyes shone with forgiveness, being gracious back was easy. "Chloe, I'm sorry—"

"No, that's okay. Nothing to apologize for. I was never much of a sister, and if you can forgive that and come to my wedding, then I can put aside the past."

Angie watched, dumbfounded, as Chloe swung her attention to Boone and regarded him with her chocolate-brown eyes. Other than her attitude, her sister hadn't changed much. She wore her straight, blond hair, so much darker than Angie's own, longer now, an inch or two past her shoulders, and she still talked with her hands. "You must be—"

"I'm Angie's valet," Boone said, lifting the two suitcases.

Chloe's merry laugh filled the air, and Angie shook her head, taking care to suppress her grin. She could feel Detry's eyes on her, and she didn't want to give him an inch when it came to showing her vulnerable spots—like Boone. No way she wanted the man to know she cared about his former lawyer.

"Warren told me all about how you believed in him," Chloe said to Boone. "Thank you."

Boone nodded once and didn't comment, but that didn't bother Chloe, who beamed at him. It was then Angie realized something that floored her.

Her sister wasn't just happy to be marrying Detry—she was euphoric. Radiant.

Oh, no. She had believed Chloe was marrying him partly for his money, but it didn't look that way. She was going to devastate her sister.

Lord, I don't want to do this anymore. Couldn't you send a miracle to save her?

As soon as she prayed it, she knew the answer. She was Chloe's miracle. Her unhappy, reluctant miracle.

"C'mon." Chloe took Angie's hand and drew her over to their mother, Madeleine, who had ventured down the steps. One more person to go. She didn't count Detry, as she could mostly safely ignore him. Chloe wouldn't notice, and her mother would be happy. Besides, Boone had moved past her and was shaking hands with his former client, so it wasn't as though Detry was being snubbed.

"Hi, Mom."

Madeleine sent her a polite, wary smile. "You're looking well, Angie."

Nothing had changed over the years she'd been gone. She could have been greeting a relative stranger, and that stung. Angie had to force herself to smile back.

This celebration was going to be worse than the thirteenth birthday party she had spent babysitting money on to buy her own decorations, refreshments and stuff to make her own cake, only to have no one come. She'd only thought that was a disaster. Now she knew what the term really meant.

Before she caved to the temptation to turn around and run right back to Boone's car, he was reaching out his hand to her mother and being charming.

"I'm Boone Walker, a friend of Angie's." He sent Angie a look that practically melted her socks off. "A really good friend."

"And Warren's lawyer, too." Madeleine's eyes softened and her shoulders relaxed as she surveyed Boone's expensive jacket. Since she'd arrived with such a "really good friend" in tow, apparently, Angie thought, her mother was no longer as worried that she'd be trying to steal a second fiancé from Chloe.

Madeleine was going to despise her by Saturday.

"I've got some dinner waiting for you if you're hungry." Madeleine flipped around and scooted up the steps and inside, with Boone following. Detry lowered and raised his head, his face unreadable, then left her and Chloe alone, closing both the screen and the main door behind them.

Chloe leaned in close and said, her voice serious, "I read about Tony's death in the papers."

Fresh pangs of regret for what she'd done hit Angie. She took a deep breath. This was so hard. She didn't have to comment, though. Chloe was already speaking.

"I know you told me you and Boone knew each other well, and Boone wanted to come. Are you two dating?"

Just like their mom, Chloe would probably feel better if she was safely "taken." Angie didn't want to lie to her, but she wasn't sure what to say. She couldn't tell her they'd been engaged, had split up and been brought together again in the face of danger— Chloe might worry that the threat followed them to her wedding, and she didn't want that.

"I wouldn't call it dating, exactly. We're extremely good friends." All she meant by that was that Boone had saved her life, and she would give hers for him if he needed her to.

Yeah, that was all.

Her sister's smile lit up her face. "He must be if he took a week off to be here with you."

"Yeah."

Chloe grabbed her arm and they started toward the porch. "We have a party with my friends tomorrow evening, the bridal shower Wednesday evening, the wedding rehearsal and dinner on Friday, and the wedding Saturday. If Boone needs to check in at his office, you'll have plenty to keep you busy."

If she only knew, Angie thought dryly. At the door, she

stopped her sister. "In the interest of total honesty, I should tell you that I testified against your fiancé at his trial."

"He told me," Chloe said matter-of-factly, her smile never fading. "I've never been a police officer—and I don't wish to be, either—so I'm not going to second-guess you on that. You did what you needed to do. There aren't any hard feelings from either of us. Anything else you're worried about?"

Yes. Oh, yes. The feeling Detry was evil and had murdered his wife that she couldn't prove. How about that?

But there was something else. "Is Mom really okay with me being here?"

"She won't talk about you," Chloe said softly, with a glance at the door, "but she agreed readily enough when I asked her if you could stay here, so let's just say yes."

That would have to be good enough for now. "How about Warren?"

Angie swore someone turned down the knob on Chloe's "bright" switch. Her sister flattened out her bottom lip for a few seconds. "No problem. He's peaceful with it."

A strange answer if she'd ever heard one. "I'm glad you found someone," Angie said. She was. She just wished it wasn't Warren Detry.

"Same here." Chloe grinned back.

"I haven't found— Oh, you mean, Boone." She kept her voice low, just in case Boone suddenly developed the ability to hear through walls. "I told you, we're just good friends."

"Let me give you a clue, Ange. A man goes to wedding festivities with you? He's more than your good friend. He's in love, whether the two of you want to admit it or not."

Boone's first love would always be the law, and there was no way she could explain that to Chloe. Her heart sinking, she realized this week was going to be even harder than she'd thought.

Awash in hearts and flowers and happy forever-afters, Chloe didn't even realize there was a "till death do you part" clause in all of that.

"How are you holding up?" Boone asked that evening.

Angie considered this. Boone had exchanged a few words about missing football with Detry, but otherwise the two men had kept to themselves, so he was keeping his promise to put her feelings first.

"All things considered, pretty well," she said, keeping her voice down so she wouldn't be overheard. It was almost eight. Chloe was seeing Warren to the door, her mother was in the kitchen doing dishes by hand and she and Boone had been left to themselves in the living room. "Detry is ignoring me, Mom is shooting me 'wish you weren't here' looks and Chloe is my new best friend."

"Replacing me?" The strange look on his face jabbed at her heart.

"Totally different category. Chloe wants to do my hair, you remind me to duck when I'm being shot at. Guess whom I couldn't live without?"

He gave her a slow grin that made her toes curl. "I gather I don't have anything to worry about."

"Unless you mess up your job." She grinned back.

Boone leaned in close, and she breathed in the scent of his woodsy aftershave that reminded her of the romantic candlelight suppers when they were dating.

She wished she could catch amnesia.

"You going to talk to your mother soon?" he asked.

"When I think it's a good time."

"Angie."

"I'm not going to lie to you," she whispered, trying to ignore the disappointment in his voice. She was actually waiting for some sign her mother would be open to conversation. Dinner had not brought one.

It had, however, eased her mind that there would be open hostility from Detry. He'd kept his eyes averted from her, just like her mother had. Apparently he shared with Angie a mutual desire not to be even hypocritically polite. It didn't matter—she still got a really bad feeling whenever he was too close. Or whenever their eyes met. Or...okay, she didn't trust the man at all, and didn't like sharing a meal with him. Not that the other two weren't trying to make it easier. Chloe had chatted, and Boone charmed, but she had been glad when the meal was over.

"I'm coping for now," she whispered. "But keep close, okay?"

"I can handle that. Trust me." His fingers covered hers, and he squeezed her hand. She didn't pull away, even though little warning flashes were lighting up in her mind. She wanted to trust him, but danger lay in letting him get too close. They had too many problems that couldn't be surmounted as long as he was so intent on controlling everything. And if she couldn't overcome the problems that had made her determined to give up motherhood, they would only make each other miserable.

But for the moment, well, sitting there with someone she knew had deep feelings for her, holding his hand, was so sweet.

Chloe breezed into the room from the kitchen. "Mom has set it up so Boone can have the downstairs guest room. It's right over there." She pointed to a closed door to the left of the short hallway leading to the kitchen. "Angie, you and I will be in my bedroom upstairs, and she'll be in hers at the head of the stairs. Want to bring your suitcase up now and see my wedding gown?"

"Yes." *No.* Angie remained seated even after her sister reached the stairs at the far side of the room.

"Go," Boone prodded quietly, his fingers moving from over hers to give her arm a gentle push.

With a sigh, she got her suitcase from the side of the stairway and climbed the stairs. She had to be careful and gain her sister's trust. Bide her time until she could figure out how to convince her sister not to marry Detry.

And pray that moment would come before it was too late.

Upstairs, Chloe was already taking a white gown from her closet and spreading it out on her four-poster twin bed. Angie gazed down at the gown. Its satin bodice had sculptured folds and drapes and small cap sleeves, and its crystal-covered full skirt glistened like freshly fallen snow.

"It's beautiful," Angie breathed, overwhelmed. She had picked a lovely creation like this for her wedding with Boone. A sigh escaped her that even Chloe heard.

"Your time will come. If ever I saw someone God picked out, it's Boone for you. You two seem perfectly attuned to each other."

"We have major problems."

"What couple doesn't?" Chloe shrugged her shoulders. "Our pastor says that's where faith and love come in."

The first time the glow had left Chloe's eyes, Angie had thought it was a fluke, but this time, her sister's words and her look came together and spoke to Angie. Could this be the evidence she needed?

"You have major problems with Det—Warren?"

"You'll work yours out with Boone," Chloe evaded. Angie didn't want to push, not yet, but alarm bells were going off. What major problems did Chloe and Detry have?

Chloe got another box from underneath her bed. Lifting the lid off, she showed Angie the crystal-covered headpiece and gossamer veil.

"Absolutely stunning."

"Warren paid for everything. I thought the money would be better off invested, but he insisted I should have a day to remember."

Still standing, Angie leaned back against the wall by the door. Her eyes took in the cot at the other end of the room, already made up with a fluffy pillow, sheets and a blanket. Chloe's way of welcoming her.

The tears, threatening all evening, almost came. She didn't want to ruin this for her sister. Or her. She wanted the cot made up with love. The smiles her sister kept sending her way. How warm it all made her feel inside.

She shut her eyes hard. She also didn't want Chloe to die.

"What made you fall in love with him?"

Chloe put the cover back on the box with the veil, her eyes bright. "His devotion to God. I couldn't marry a man who wasn't devoted to the Lord."

Thinking of Boone, Angie's heart thumped painfully. "Surely there must have been other men at church who were devoted *and* interested in you." Without being so much older.

"His focus is different from the other men I've met. He wants to set up a mission to help the poor. Since he has already made a fortune, we don't have to worry about making money, so I can quit my job if I want."

Part of Detry's fortune was made with his dead wife's insurance money. Angie shoved away a sick sensation, and focused on her sister. She wasn't surprised Chloe would choose a wealthy man to marry, but she was surprised she would quit her own career. Her sister loved to work. Or more precisely, she loved to make money. Being secure was everything to her.

"Are you really considering quitting your job?" Angie sat on the bed and trailed her fingers over the softness of the gown as her sister watched her.

Again, Chloe hesitated. "I don't know. I just finished putting myself through college, and my boss is talking about a promotion." She rounded the bed and came back over to sit by Angie. "I'll tell you, no matter what a man promises you, you shouldn't depend only on him. I learned that when Dad died and

Mom found out he'd let his insurance policy lapse. I don't want to end up like her, worried about the next dime if something happens to Warren."

Something happens to Warren... An unseemly comment sprang to the tip of her tongue, but Angie firmly closed her lips. She was supposed to be thinking Christian-like thoughts, not human ones.

That Chloe had at least one toe on the ground when it came to Detry was good. It would make her fall to earth just a little easier when she finally got the evidence she needed.

Major problems with Detry, Chloe had said. She needed to remember to find out what those were.

"What I love most of all about Warren is how much he wants a child. He didn't have much of a family growing up in Colleyville, and that's all he ever wanted, he said."

Eerie, Angie thought, how much Detry's heartfelt desire to have a family echoed her own, only in a different way, and Boone's, in the exact same. Was God trying to get her to see Detry as a human being much like herself?

She shuddered inwardly.

"What made you fall in love with Boone?" Chloe asked.

Chloe's question made her put away her own. For now, anyway. "We're not in love." At least she didn't think she was, not since he'd put his client before her. "Just good friends, remember?"

"Okay, then what made you fall into 'good friends' with him?"

She didn't even have to think to describe the heady days of falling in love with Boone. The words flowed. "He treated me like I was the most special person in his whole life. He made me a part of his. When I'm irritated, or down, he can make me laugh my way right out of my mood."

Chloe grinned. "Oh, nothing there to actually *love,* I see."

"And he's an eye magnet," she said, quoting Ida.

They looked at each other and giggled simultaneously.

"That was a shallow thing for a Christian to list, wasn't it?"

"If he was a bad person, would you still think he was good-looking?"

"Probably not." Angie's lips lifted at the sides. "Maybe."

Giggling again, Chloe rose to her feet and lifted the dress by the hanger, high in the air, so she could drape the skirt over her other arm. For a moment, Angie put aside all her worries. If she ever married anyone—which was looking less and less likely—she wanted an iridescent skirt that flowed like that. It shimmered as Chloe raised the material, her arm high enough for her wide, short sleeve to fall backward…

Yellow bruises appeared in a line on Chloe's upper arm.

Angie's heart stopped. She'd seen fingertip shaped bruises like that at least fifty times, maybe more, on victims of domestic abuse. Sometimes children, but mostly women.

"Chloe, those bruises—"

"I know." Her sister blushed. "I'm hoping they'll disappear by Saturday." Keeping the dress off the rug, Chloe walked to the closet, not offering any information.

"Did Warren do that?" The question came out sharper than she intended.

Chloe finished hanging the dress, shut the white paneled closet door, and headed back to Angie, her cheeks even pinker. "He had to grab me to keep me from crossing in front of someone who ran a red light when we were leaving a restaurant in Cincinnati. I slipped, and he pulled harder to keep me from falling. I bruise easily. Believe me, it's not going to happen again."

As a patrol officer who answered domestic calls, Angie had heard the excuses almost as many times as she'd seen the bruises. Her heart beat faster. This was her evidence. God had known it was right here.

"Chloe, everything I know and have seen as a cop says that domestic abuse doesn't get better. It escalates. This time he gripped you too tightly, next time he might slap you, after that a punch and kick. And he'll blame you—"

"I *told* you, it was an accident," Chloe interrupted, her eyes zeroing in on her, her formerly sunny face darkening. "Please don't make a big deal about it. I'm very happy, and I don't want anything spoiling that."

Shutting up went against everything Angie stood for, but Chloe wasn't ready to hear anything against Detry. Without other proof that he really was evil, and with Chloe in denial about the bruises, Angie knew she could be asked to leave if she pushed.

So she closed her mouth. But not her heart. Not this time. Getting up, Angie rounded the bed, and reached out to hug Chloe. Chloe hugged her back, apparently not taking offense.

This time.

That night, the more Angie thought about the bruises on her sister's arm, the more certain she became that she had to do something fast. Chloe and Madeleine were both working through Wednesday, so she'd have two days free.

What she came up with would upset Boone's apple cart. Not that she minded doing that. It was alienating him totally she couldn't afford to do. With Detry so close, and whoever else was out there wanting to blow her head off as far as she knew, she needed Boone.

And wasn't that a habit she needed to break?

From the second Angie swept into the kitchen the next morning, Boone knew they were going to have a problem. She was dressed in jeans and an emerald T-shirt that set off the green in her eyes perfectly. Those weren't unusual. What tipped him off to trouble was the brown suede blazer, on a warm June day.

She was carrying.

"What have you got planned?" he asked, his eyes narrowing.

"Chloe and Mom just left for work, right?" She went right to the cupboard with the supermarket china in it, Boone noted. Apparently Madeleine had not changed her habits much in the years Angie had been gone.

"That's what they said, yes."

"Good." She filled her cup and left it black, carrying it over to the table and sitting next to him. "I have a plan, and I don't want them to hear it."

"You have a plan and a gun. To tell you the truth, I don't think I want to hear it, either." He'd been working on some files from his office, but he didn't suppose he would get any more work done anytime soon. He pressed a few buttons to shut down his laptop.

"That's fine with me." She sipped some coffee, put down the cup, and held out her hand, palm open. "Just let me borrow your car for a while. I need to go someplace."

He couldn't help it. He started laughing. "It ain't happening. I'm your bodyguard, remember? Where you go, I go."

"You're my bodyguard, not my husband."

He stopped laughing. His royal-blue eyes penetrated into hers. "I'm still sorry about that."

She blinked her eyes. Maybe she should say she was sorry about bringing it up. Maybe. If he gave her the keys.

He didn't. She pulled her hand back and swallowed her apology. "Fine. I'll take a cab to the nearest rent-a-wreck and get a car myself."

"That ain't happening, either. I'll drive you wherever you want to go. Remember the men in the Mustang who mistook you for one of those paper doll targets? They're still out there, as of this morning. You die, I'll never get over it."

"Honest?" That shouldn't stop her momentum, but it did.

"Do I ever say anything I don't mean?"

"No, you don't." Their gazes held for a long moment. He was trying, she'd give him that. She prayed one day she'd be able to look at him and not automatically worry he would shove her aside for someone else's interests, but she didn't hold out much hope.

Sometimes she hated being her.

"It's best I go alone," she said. "You aren't going to want to drive me when you find out what I'm up to anyway."

"Sure I will. It's preferable to you ending up dead."

She drew in a deep breath. "I have to go to the town Detry told Chloe he grew up in. Talk to people who knew him. See if he had a reputation for any kind of violence as a youth."

His scowl told Angie he wasn't liking what he was hearing. "Look, this guy had the misfortune to have his wife murdered. He is not going to hurt your sister."

"He already did. He put bruises on Chloe's arm."

The sudden concern in his eyes was encouraging. "How do you know?" he asked.

She told him what she'd seen. "Chloe said it wasn't his fault. He yanked her back from going in front of a car that ran a red and gripped too hard."

"Well, then…"

"She also said she bruises easily," she added.

Even he recognized a woman defending a man's bad behavior when he heard it. She could tell by the disgusted way he shook his head. "She's making excuses."

"That's been my experience in domestic-violence cases I've handled."

"It could have just been accidental."

"There's something else you don't know. The town he told you he grew up in? The one he checked out fine in? That was Butterfield. But Detry told Chloe he grew up in Colleyville.

Either he was lying to her, or he lied to you. I want to go there and find out."

Boone closed the lid to his laptop. "If we don't find anything, will you drop all of this and start focusing on your own happiness?"

"Sure." Easy to promise. They were going to find something out, she was positive of it. Detry had lied about his hometown, and he wouldn't have done that unless he had a reason.

EIGHT

East of Copper City, Colleyville had a boarded-up shop for every open one, and there were only a few of those. The very few people Boone and Angie could find had never heard of Warren Detry. They had no luck at the library with old newspapers, either. They'd been wiped out in a huge fire in 1983 that had taken out the town's former library; a factory, its main source of income; and some homes. But the librarian did give them a name and address to try.

Angie and Boone found retired area doctor, Theodore Willoughby, fishing at a man-made pond on his huge estate, several yards downhill from his house. He was a big man with a gray beard and wire-rimmed glasses, who loved to talk.

Her kind of man, Angie thought.

"Troublemaker older teenage boys in the late seventies? Sure. The drugs started coming into town then, and we had our share like anywhere. But no Warren Detry."

"How about teenagers arrested for battery on women?" Angie asked. That could be another way of finding Detry.

He shook his head. "Back then, I might have suspected a woman was beaten when I treated her, but I can't recall ever having one admit she was." He rubbed his fingers through his beard. "Sorry I couldn't help."

"Thanks anyway." Angie handed him a slip of paper with her name and cell-phone number on it. "If you think of something that might help us, please do call, okay? This guy might be dangerous, and he's about to marry my sister."

She turned and started walking up the hill, Boone right beside her.

"I can't believe God would lead me on this dead end. Why would Detry lie to my sister and say this was his hometown, Boone? It doesn't make sense. Unless—"

"—unless he changed his name at some point and they know him as someone else here," Boone filled in.

"You mean, he might have *lied?* Not to you," she teased. She couldn't help it.

Boone didn't crack under the pressure. "If he lived here under a different name, there would be no record of his arrests under the name Detry, and therefore, no evidence here you can use—unless you can tie him to his name of birth.

"And before you consider that," he added, "investigating a name change is a nightmare. They can be changed legally, anywhere, at any time." He paused. "Unless it's for crime-related purposes."

She raised her eyebrow at him. "Exactly."

"Hey!" Dr. Willoughby boomed from the bottom of the hill. "I thought of something!"

They turned simultaneously. The elderly man was trudging up the path, and they hurried down to meet him. He smiled his thanks as he leaned over, placed a hand above either knee, and took a long, deep breath.

Straightening, he peered over his wire-rim glasses. "Sorry about that. I would stay in better shape, but hey, I'm retired. Nothing much hereabouts to do except go fishing and visit my lady friend down in Dawson."

The edges of Angie's lips lifted. The doc had to be in his seventies. This time, Boone elbowed her.

"You wanted to tell us something?" she asked.

"Sure do. Since it's life and death and all, why don't you try asking my lady friend? She lived up here in Colleyville for years. Only moved down to Dawson to keep her job after the fire." He gave them directions that were simple enough Angie didn't even have to write them down. "Can't miss it. It's a biker bar. Her name's Ida."

Stunned, Angie's mouth dropped open. She glanced at Boone, who shook his head. *Don't let on*, his eyes said.

"You look surprised," Doc Willoughby said.

"Just that a retired doctor would date someone in a biker bar," Angie said. Doc Willoughby with Ida. The Lord was amazing.

He smiled. "Not so surprising. I used to own a hog. Powerful, noisy, expensive bike. Ida has one, too."

That had to be their Ida. "That's nice you have someone," she told the doctor. "Is there a wedding in the future?"

"I'm thinking probably not. Ida's playing hard to get. Moved away for a while and wouldn't tell me why. Right now, we're just good friends."

"I know how that goes," Angie said, glancing at Boone.

"Make sure you don't mention my name, okay?" The doctor frowned. "She's had some trouble and won't even answer my calls. I'm lying low until she remembers what she's missing."

"Gotcha." The two of them took off, moving fast. Just in case their voices drifted down the hill, Angie held off saying anything else until they were in the Mercedes.

"We really need to get that disk Ida took with her. And to find out why she's running. Because she knows something, Boone." She could feel it.

"I totally agree," Boone said. "How lucky are we Doc Willoughby is irritated with her and won't be calling to warn her we're coming so she can disappear again?"

"Seriously, I don't think luck has anything to do with it." Angie unbuttoned her blazer and unsnapped her shoulder holster. "You're carrying, right?"

"When I'm with you, of course." He patted his jacket.

She gave him a poison-laced smile. He grinned back and added, "If it isn't just luck we happened upon Ida, and it is God directing us now, then why worry about weapons?"

She hesitated, unsure. "Just in case one of the bikers gets a hold of Ida's bat, takes exception to your sense of humor, and wants to take a swing at you. If you want a more spiritually based answer, I'm afraid I don't have one right now."

"Naw, that one will work just fine."

She smiled up at him. "I'm glad you're helping me, Boone. It's just that sometimes you make me forget how happy I am to know you."

He chuckled, but then his face went serious. "Maybe you should stay outside while I go in."

"Funny, I was thinking I might have a better chance of getting through the bikers to Ida than you. Being female and all. Plus, you're more irritating than I am."

"Yeah, but Ida likes me better."

"Only because you're an eye magnet." She grinned.

"Let's just see what we're up against when we get there."

"Deal." Angie bowed her head, closed her eyes and said a quick prayer they wouldn't be up against anything.

The biker bar was nestled in the trees just off the main highway, probably on purpose, Boone noticed, so the bikes wouldn't disturb homeowners and cause lawsuits. He parked just inside the gravel parking lot to avoid scratches on his car and surveyed what they would be up against.

There were only three bikes in front of the long, autumn-red building. Slow day. Still…

"Maybe I ought to go in the front and you stay around back."

"I feel my blood pressure rising, Boone." Angie ran her finger around the edge of her T-shirt collar, pulling it away from her neck. "You still aren't taking my capabilities as a cop seriously."

"Sure I am." He loved watching her dramatics, but she was wrong. "If I wasn't, I'd tie you up and leave you here where I know you'll be safe."

"My hero," she said, her mouth twisting with mirth.

"I try," he said modestly. "So you figure she's got the disk, do you?"

"Where would you keep it if you were a woman in her sixties? In a vulnerable apartment where you lived alone, or in a building with guys who ride those?" She pointed to the bikes.

"You're asking *me* how women think?"

They both chuckled at that as they got out of the car and headed for the front door of the bar, their steps crunching in the gravel lot.

Boone moved his jaw from side to side. Angie didn't have the qualms about this he had. She'd prayed and was fine because she had faith. He, however, didn't want to let his guard down.

Maybe it was being around a praying woman so much, he didn't know, but as Angie pulled open the heavy front door, he muttered a quick prayer for the first time in years that God would keep her safe. All that came to him afterward was that God would—through him. He wasn't sure the prayer had made a difference.

Boone slipped inside the bar first. Angie knew he was doing it to protect her, so she didn't protest. It was funny in a way—because now she was covering his back, and he didn't even realize it.

A golden oldies rock song blared from a stereo hooked to two small speakers. Her eyebrows raised. Not what she was expecting. Neither were the two lone bikers, both of whom had definitely been adults when the song was a contemporary hit.

"Is this a biker bar, or a retirement haven?" Boone whispered in her ear.

She stifled the laughter that sprang to her lips when the two bikers stood. Their expressions didn't look like they thought *they* were funny.

"You two a little lost?" one asked, raising his gravelly voice to be heard over the music.

"Doc Willoughby sent us," Angie said, eyeing them right back. "We're looking for Ida."

The one with a long ponytail tied at his nape and muscular arms that would rival any bodybuilder's kept his eyes pinned on Angie. If he knew Doc Willoughby, he wasn't letting on.

"Ida isn't here," he said shortly.

Angie gazed down at the small table next to them with the two beer mugs and a paperback nonfiction bestseller about modern-day murderers behind bars. Bingo.

"Sure she is," she said. "Three bikes, two bikers, you do the math. And you two don't seem like the types to read while you drink."

"Appearances can be deceiving."

Boone decided to skip the polite chatter. "Ida? It's the eye magnet," he called loudly. "You here?"

"Were you followed?" Ida's voice responded loudly.

"No," Angie said. "Boone, the bar is talking."

"You're not dragging me back to Copper City," it said.

Angie and Boone shared a surprised look. "No problem," Angie assured her. "Ida, I feel funny talking to a bar."

Frosted hair and a set of pale green eyes peeked over the counter's edge, then Ida raised herself into view. "About time you found me." She hurried to the stereo, turned it down and gestured for Angie and Boone to come to the bar. "It's safe," she told the two men. "They're good friends, like I said."

The two men whom Ida introduced as Rick and Micah nodded, and then carried their drinks to separate windows and settled on chairs. From their vantage points, they pretty much could cover most of the lot and see who was coming. Not one hundred percent fail safe, Angie thought, but not bad.

"Why didn't you let us know you were going into hiding, Ida?" She sat on a bar stool. "We were worried about you."

Ida's eyes softened considerably. "Sorry about that. I had to get someplace I knew I would be safe."

To her amazement, Angie was feeling a rush of happiness at seeing Ida again, something she'd only experienced before with Boone—and not her own mother.

"I thought you retired from this job," Angie said.

"I did. I'm half owner of the place now."

Interesting that in giving Boone her life story, the other woman hadn't bothered to mention she'd managed to save enough to buy into the bar, which was a pretty nice establishment—for a beer joint. She'd been in a few to arrest drunks for disorderly conduct, so she had firsthand knowledge.

Ida dipped two glasses in ice, then poured ginger-ale in them. "Here. All this detective work finding me must have made you thirsty." She raised her head and got the bikers' attention. "Keep your eyes open, boys. Somebody could have followed my friends."

"No one knows we're in the area," Angie told her.

"No offense, honey, but how do you stay alive, thinking like that?"

Boone chuckled. She scowled at him.

"If you own the place, what were you doing working at the cemetery?" Boone asked.

"A death watch." Ida folded her arms across her chest. "You two don't need to know more than that."

Angie took a sip of the icy ginger-ale, put her drink down and smiled to diffuse the sudden tension between Ida's side of the counter and theirs.

"Don't worry, we're only here to get the surveillance disk from the cemetery you have. The sheriff's department needs it. They're investigating who shot at Boone and me the day we met you, and who showed up to hurt you. They're hoping to find evidence on the footage."

The way Ida's keen eyes speculated, Angie wondered if the woman knew something they didn't. "Doc Willoughby say anything about me?"

Angie smiled, pleased to tell her. "He misses you a lot."

Ida lit up like one of the neon signs in her window, but only for a few seconds. "How did you convince Teddy to say where I was?"

Angie splayed her fingers outward in question. "All I told him was that the guy we were asking him about was dangerous and about to marry my sister. He said to ask you for the information we needed, but you already said you didn't know anything about Warren Detry."

"That's what I said, all right." But Ida's face had paled while Angie spoke. She was lying.

"So, as I said, we came for the surveillance footage that was missing out of your apartment."

Ida reached over to a box of potato chips on a shelf, pulled out a bag and tore a piece of clear tape off the top of the back. From that she pulled out a DVD case, brushed it off and handed it to Boone.

"I would have never have guessed," Boone said.

"I figured nobody but a really hungry perp would have looked in there, so it'd be safe." Ida smiled, pleased to be complimented.

Angie watched Boone put the disk inside a pocket in his jacket and wondered how she could get more information about Detry out of Ida. Behind them, the bikers shifted around, but no one came inside the bar.

"Did you watch what's on it, Ida?" she asked, eyeing Boone. He seemed willing to wait, picking up his glass and taking a drink as if he didn't care what Ida said. Yeah. Same as her.

Ida nodded. "That grave you two looked at? There was a lot of activity around there. Make sure the good guys get it, okay?"

"We will." Boone stood and gave her another of his business cards. "It shouldn't be long before word gets out the law has the disk now, and you shouldn't have to worry about the guys in the Mustang anymore."

"We can handle them." Ida waved her hand at the bikers. "You two best be getting along before the afternoon crowd gets here. You'll be bad for business."

"This isn't your afternoon crowd?" Angie asked with a wave of her hand.

"You kidding?" Ida scoffed. "Rick and Micah are my posse."

Angie bit into her lip to keep from laughing. Boone managed to keep his face entirely straight as he took out his wallet to pay for the drinks. How, she didn't know. Posse. Ahem.

Ida shook her head at Boone's money. "It's on me." She rounded the end of the bar again and walked them to the door. "Don't be strangers."

Then Ida did the strangest thing. She reached out and enveloped Angie in a quick, tight hug that left her open-mouthed. Ida didn't seem to notice.

"Get out of here," the bar owner said, "and go save your sister." She turned to Boone. "Take good care of her."

"Yes, ma'am."

Dazed, Angie followed Boone outside the building. As soon

as they were a few feet from the door, Angie moved closer to Boone and whispered, "What on earth just happened?"

"She hugged you."

"But why?" Angie gazed all around them as they walked back toward Boone's rental. "Ida doesn't seem like the hugging type."

"You must have tugged at her heartstrings." Boone's royal blue eyes twinkled. "You tug at mine."

"You're doing that sweet thing again," she said. "I'm starting to like it, but stop. It's distracting."

"You're really starting to like it?"

"I never stopped." Oops, too much sharing with him. That was not good. Nor would looking at his face right now be good, because she didn't want to melt. She needed to get her focus off him. "But right now, I have my sister's life to think about."

He sighed.

"Boone. Focus. Something is all off with Ida." She stopped at the car and looked at him over the roof. "She took a job at the cemetery doing a 'death watch'. Watching for death. Was she expecting someone to die and be brought to the Last Stop?" Her eyes widened in horror. "Cliff?"

"I don't think so." Boone gave a slow shake of his head. He scanned the area, ever watchful. "I think it's simpler than that. Maybe she was waiting for a certain person to visit one of the graves. That's why she needed the disks—so she could check night footage."

"Yeah, but whose grave? Laurie Detry's? Come to think of it, she never did have to check the map like she said. She knew exactly where it was. We've got to get back and view that disk."

She opened the door and slid inside. When he got in, he wore a "you aren't going to like this" expression.

"You realize there could be quite a lot of viewing time on this disk?" he asked. "By the time we get back to your mom's, they could be home from work. With the engagement party tonight, we won't get another chance to view it until Chloe and your mom go to work tomorrow. We'd learn more, faster, if we drop it off at Jack's on the way home."

"And you two can conveniently keep me from knowing what you find out?" She shook her head and clamped her arms over her chest. "I want to see it."

"Maybe we can fit in watching some of it at Jack's."

"I can cancel our going to the party, and we can watch it all."

"You'll need a good excuse."

"Saving Chloe's life?" she asked, then regretted the sarcastic edge to the words.

He just shook his head. Reaching over her, he put the disk in the glove compartment, found a small key on his ring and locked it. His way of ensuring she wouldn't snatch the footage and keep him from doing what he wanted.

Her lips pursed together. He was asking for trouble.

Irritated as she was, she started watching out around them as they turned onto the country road, something she'd been doing constantly since the car chase. Not two hundred yards from the bar, she spotted a red car parked down an old access road, and her heart skipped a beat.

"The Mustang," she said, pointing.

Boone quickly found a place to turn around and headed back to the bar at breakneck speed. His wheels squealed with his sudden turn into the parking lot. Jamming on his brakes, he cut the motor and reached for the cell phone in his pocket. Her gun ready, Angie opened the door.

"Hold on," Boone ordered. "I'm calling Jack."

"You hold on. I'm going in." Ida and the posse could be in danger. She wasn't chancing it. Besides, she wanted these guys captured.

Boone hit the shortcut key, then launched himself from the car. He stopped long enough to tell Jack the problem and their location, then slipped the phone into his pocket and took off after Angie with Jack hanging on the line. She was leaning against the outside wall next to a window, out of eyeshot of anyone inside. Her lips moved, although she didn't say a word.

Prayer again.

"I've called for help," he said in an urgent whisper, leaning against the rust-painted wood.

Angie edged herself over, took a quick look through the window, then turned back to him. "Looks like Micah has a gun on one man, and he's got his hands up in the air. I don't see a second."

She was right. He lifted the phone and warned Jack about the Mustang's possibly having a second suspect in it. Then he looked at Angie. "You want to check the back, or go inside?"

"The back."

The riskier option. Of course.

He headed toward the front door to brace himself on the far side of it. "It's Boone," he yelled, then turned the knob and pulled on the door handle. He stayed back to one side as it swung open, just in case. But no one shot.

The biker with the long hair, Rick, filled the doorway. "C'mon in. Ida's fine."

"Angie's checking the back. There still might be another guy out there," Boone warned.

"Not according to him," Rick said, indicating the man they'd captured, who was prone on the floor with Micah's boot on his back and a shotgun pointed at him.

"The back's locked up," Angie said, coming in the front door. She stared down at the man on the floor. He'd been the one shooting at them.

"His name is Clive Thatcher," Rick said, indicating a battered wallet on the bar counter. "We checked his ID—just in case he managed to get away."

"Quit squirming," Micah told their captive.

"You're hurting me," Thatcher growled.

Boone strode over to him, crouched down, and lifted the guy's head backward by his hair. "You tried to kill us, you came after a defenseless old lady—"

"Hey!" Ida protested.

"—and you're whining? Who sent you?"

"Nobody."

Boone stood up and looked at Micah. "Shoot him."

As a Christian and a cop, she should protest their trying to scare Thatcher into talking without his rights, Angie thought. She should. But when it was her life on the line, where was it drawn? Or was it drawn at all?

Micah pressed the shotgun against Thatcher's back and repeated Boone's question.

"I can't tell you!" Thatcher protested. "He'll kill me if I talk. He already killed Ed."

Boone regarded him with the coldest stare Angie had ever seen coming from him. "You get a chance to talk to the coward who hired you, tell him to leave Ida alone. She doesn't have what he wants anymore. I do."

Backing off and gesturing for Micah to let up on the shotgun, Boone tried to shake off the anger pulsing through his muscles. He shifted his attention to the bar, where Ida was staring speculatively at him.

"Sorry about the defenseless crack, Ida."

She grinned at him leaving out the "old" part. "Now I see why Angie likes you so much."

"Only sometimes," Angie said, handing Rick the cuffs she had in her handbag. As he secured their captive, Micah grinned at her.

"Still think we're over the hill?"

Angie looked from one biker to the other and shook her head. "No, but I'm beginning to wonder if I wandered into another dimension."

"I always feel that way when I leave the church and come here," Rick said.

Angie's eyebrows raised.

"I'm a pastor at the Colleyville Community Church," Rick told her, extending his hand. "We have the afternoon shift to protect Ida, but I'm over here a lot anyway doing a biker's ministry."

Angie glanced at their tables. The two mugs of beer were still full, and the napkins under them sopping, showing they had been sitting there a while.

"They're just for show," Micah said.

Ida rounded the bar to join them, her eyes on Angie. "Rick and Micah were Green Berets in Vietnam. Told you I could count on the bikers to protect me." She patted Rick's shoulder, and he grinned at her.

"Yeah, you did." And she, Angie thought, had jumped to a wrong conclusion thinking God didn't have a hand in arranging Ida's posse.

If she could be wrong concerning God about that, what else was she wrong about? Watching Boone trample Thatcher's legal rights and not stepping in worried her. Was she, like Boone, doing the wrong thing herself, trying to nuke the happiness of a man she couldn't even prove was guilty of anything? Maybe God wasn't leading her after all. Maybe she was trying to take justice into her own hands, like Boone just had.

Walking over to a small table, she sank down into the chair, lowered her head and asked God for a sign of which way to go to save her sister. When she opened her eyes, she found Rick across from her. Boone was standing with Ida, talking, and Micah was still guarding the prisoner.

"Figured you might like some company," Rick said. "So I prayed for what you're praying for."

"Answers from God?"

"No." Rick shook his head. "I prayed for you to have peace—that's what you want from God. You want answers, go to Ida."

Was that her sign? Angie gazed from Rick to Ida and back again. His eyes were so sure. She glanced at Ida again. What secrets was she hiding that everyone seemed to know but her? She needed to find out.

Jack arrived then with a deputy, and everything got busy for a while. The area and the Mustang were searched, and a body tentatively identified as Ed Northrup was found in the trunk. Thatcher clammed up and was taken away. Finally, Boone disappeared outside with Jack, going to make certain Ed Northrup was the second Mustang shooter. That was when Angie grabbed Ida's arm and dragged her to the ladies' room, where she was certain they wouldn't be disturbed.

"I need to know who's on that disk," she said.

"Sure, hon. Two men came to that grave you dug next to. The Detry grave. One was Warren Detry. The other man, he came later—I honestly don't know who he is."

Angie's nerves jumped like popcorn kernels over a growing fire. "But you knew who Warren Detry was?"

"I did." Ida's eyes searched hers. She was waiting for her to say something, Angie realized.

"How did you know?"

"I was investigating him. I saw Detry's picture in the paper when he was on trial, waited at the courthouse until he came out one day and followed him to the cemetery. A regular visitor, that one."

Angie's breath caught. Ida had a personal connection with Detry.

"I lucked out and got a job at Last Stop so I could follow him home and keep an eye on him sometimes. But he never went anywhere except to church events with your sister. I was about to give up trailing him when you and the eye magnet showed up, and then I got some sense whacked into me by that hoodlum Thatcher. I figured he was warning me to cut ties with you, so I did. Been lying low here in Dawson until I can figure out my next step."

"Why were you investigating him?" Angie asked, her pulse racing. "Who do you think Detry really is, Ida?"

Ida's mouth moved from side to side as she struggled with telling her. "I think he's the man who murdered my daughter and then burned down her house and a whole street in Colleyville to cover it up. So he could get away."

Angie's mouth dropped open. The fire the librarian had mentioned. Arson? After murdering Ida's daughter? Detry would go to jail forever.

"But I can't be sure," Ida added quickly. "The name's different. It was so many years ago. He's much older, and his face is different, too, somehow. My daughter was angry with me and had moved out. I only met Detry a few times. One time when she said they were getting married, right before she died." She took a tissue out of her pocket and wiped her eyes.

"But you think this guy and Detry might be the same man?" Angie asked.

She nodded slowly. "I believe he found out I was trying to get something on him to prove his guilt, and he sent that man in there. To scare me away the first time. But this time, to get the evidence, he said, and kill me."

"But Rick and Micah were here." Angie was so glad. Then she realized what Ida had said. "If Detry sent Thatcher, I wonder why he wants the disk."

"Maybe he's tied to the other man on it. Don't know. I was

gonna mail that disk to the eye magnet, you know, but I was in such a tizzy, I forgot his name."

Angie tilted her head, grinning.

"Hey, you try being 68. You'll be forgetting the eye magnet's name, too."

"There are times I want to, Ida."

"Men can be like that." Ida whooshed out a breath. "Don't know why this 'Detry' didn't just have me killed the first time he had a chance. But maybe he's playing games with me. Killers like that have funny reasons for doing stuff, you know. I've been reading up on the criminal mind, trying to guess his next move."

That explained her choice of reading material. "You're amazing, Ida."

"Thank you. It's harder than I thought it would be, this investigating stuff. There's no witnesses to where the fire started. Nothing Detry is doing wrong. Nothing but a name change, and that's not illegal."

"Unless it's done to hide from the law," Angie pointed out. "What is his real name?"

"If it's the same man, he grew up in Colleyville as Wayne Donaldson."

Wayne Donaldson. "What makes you think he and Warren are the same man?"

"This Detry looks just like Donaldson's father did at that age. And his eyes. You look at him, and you don't feel comfortable. I'll never forget Wayne's eyes." She shook her head. "I guess it's silly to focus on that."

"No, Ida, I don't think it's silly at all. I've experienced the same thing."

Ida just looked at her with a world-weariness that felt familiar to Angie. So now she knew for certain "Detry" was a false name. That explained a lot. If he hadn't had a slip of the tongue over his hometown, they would never have gotten this far. But still, it wasn't proof.

"Don't worry," she told Ida. "You're not alone fighting Detry anymore. I'm after him. You believe Detry killed your daughter. I still think he murdered Laurie Detry, and that evidence we found doesn't totally rule him out."

Ida looked shocked, and Angie pounced on that. "Please, please come with me and talk to my sister about what you suspect, before she marries him."

"I don't want to go near that man again," Ida said. "He just tried to have me killed. I got…a reason to stay alive."

Doc Willoughby, she probably meant. Angie had once felt that way about Boone. No, too sad. She refocused.

"Chloe's bridal shower is tomorrow evening, just outside of Cincinnati." She found a piece of paper and scribbled down the time and the name of the small country club where it would be held. "Detry won't be there. Can you come then?"

"She's not going to listen to me, a total stranger. Besides, I'm not sure they're the same man."

Every instinct told Angie they were, and she couldn't let Ida leave while she was still wavering. "Chloe's smart, Ida. If you tell her what you told me, she'll listen." She prayed she would, anyway. "You're the only chance I have at this point."

"I'll think on it." Ida headed to the door, then turned. "If I do come, I'm bringing my posse for protection."

"Absolutely." This time, Angie noticed, Ida did not hug her as she left.

Closing her eyes, she sank against the air-conditioned, cold tiles of the ladies'-room wall. If Chloe didn't believe Ida, she was going to hate Angie, and she would be finished at the house. Without saving Chloe, and without having spoken with her mother.

Tomorrow was going to be make or break. After that, she was

out of options, with only two days left before the nuptials. Ida had to be the answer to her prayer.

In the meantime, she had to decide whether or not to clue Boone in on what was up with Ida. Ida was on the edge. One word from the eye magnet, and Ida would never come, either from respect or just plain having a crush on Boone. Angie knew that. If she could convince Boone to stay neutral, the problem wouldn't arise, but she doubted he would. Ida's slight uncertainty about Donaldson being Detry would be enough to send up red flags for him.

On the other hand, with Boone watching her for signs she was living her faith, she didn't want to be secretive and evasive with him about anything.

She shoved through the bathroom door and walked into the bar just in time to see Boone give Jack the disk. Her shoulders drooped. She'd thought he was putting her first, but no. If Boone thought it would be better for her not to know, she'd never find out who the second man was on the footage. Jack's loyalty was to Boone, not her. He wouldn't talk. She was on her own in her venture to bring down Detry.

So be it. Boone could bask in ignorance about Ida for all she cared.

NINE

After only an hour of giggling women, lacy streamers and rose and white balloons at the bridal shower—not to mention the glares Angie sent his way—Boone wished he had brought his laptop so he could escape to the quiet hall to work. He'd given the surveillance footage to Jack the day before, and you didn't get madder than Angie had been on the drive back to Madeleine's.

What he'd done made sense, though. With the two of them relatively safe in Newton now that the Mustang gunmen were out of the way, and with Jack doing the detective work concerning the cemetery footage, Angie would be free to work on her relationship with her family—especially her mother.

Apparently, though, she was not seeing things his way. She sent him another dark look, then returned her attention to her sister, who was opening presents in the front of the room to applause and more giggles.

He leaned down and said quietly, "You can cheer up. Making me come here with you was great revenge."

He was close enough to smell her honeysuckle perfume. He loved that flower. When he got back home, he was going to plant bushes of honeysuckle.

Man, he could deny it all he wanted, but he had it bad for Angie.

"Who said I made you come for revenge?" she asked with a sweet smile.

"If not for revenge, then why am I here?"

"To watch my back, of course." She smiled again and returned to watching her sister.

Her gaze kept wandering toward the door as if she wanted to escape…or was waiting for someone. The same inner alarm he used to tell whether a prospective client was guilty clanged now. She wasn't telling him something.

He thought back over the day before. After Rick had told him Ida and Angie were talking, Ida had exploded out of the bathroom into the bar and left on her bike, and a minute or so later, Angie had appeared with a determined look on her face. He wasn't sure what that look meant then, but now he wondered if Ida had told her something she could use to break up the wedding and Angie had made a plan. That could be what Angie was keeping from him.

He shifted his gaze back to her. She was focused on Chloe, a slight frown on her lips now. Was her troubled look over Chloe's choice of groom—or was it from remembering they'd been this close to their own wedding not so long ago? It had to bother her, sitting through this.

It was bothering him.

She rose to get some of the lemon punch. In indigo blue with her blond hair and lovely face, Angie stood out as brilliantly from the other women there as the sun peeking through gray clouds would.

He sucked in a breath. With each new day he spent with Angie, his emotions got more and more tangled up in her. Even now, he had to remind himself they were too different and couldn't give each other what they wanted. None of that, however, stopped his heart from wanting her in his life.

Chloe's mother announced the next game at the same time Boone's cell phone vibrated in his shirt pocket. Jack's number showed on the screen. He pressed the keypad and held the phone to his ear, slipping off the cushioned chair to walk toward the doorway so he could hear better, fully aware that Angie was following him. He knew every move she made when she was around. Instinctively.

"Jack. Finally. Thought you'd never call."

Jack chuckled. "I wouldn't think being in the middle of a bunch of women in their twenties and thirties would be that much of a hardship."

"They're about to play some bridal-shower game called 'How to Hook and Catch a Single Man'. I'll never look at fishing the same way again."

Angie could only hear snatches of Boone's conversation as she traced his steps through the doorway, into the hall and down to a love seat that she refused to sit on with him. Silly, maybe, but it was the principle.

Boone gazed up at her as he listened to Jack, his easy-going look suddenly changing as anger streaked through him.

"Was Karen hurt?" he asked into the phone.

Karen, his secretary. Something to do with his office? Angie waited a couple of minutes as Boone listened, then tapped his arm and raised her eyebrows at him in question. He told Jack to hang on.

"A man came into my office around one this afternoon and pulled a gun on Karen. He tied her up and ransacked every place that could be searched. She's all right. He didn't say what he was looking for."

"Identity?"

Boone shook his head. "He wore a mask. She called the local police, but didn't tell them where we are."

He only spent a couple more minutes on the phone, then hung up. His eyes were grave.

"They ruled Cliff's death a homicide."

Angie took a sharp breath and sank onto the seat next to him. Principles be hanged. "I knew it. I knew Cliff wouldn't take his own life."

"The funeral is tomorrow morning at ten, Victory Community Church in Copper City, but after this break-in, Jack and I don't think it will be safe for you to go."

"I have to." She needed to tell Cliff goodbye.

The look Boone gave her was so familiar. It was the same one Ida's eyes had had the day before when she considered how much information to spill.

"Jack thinks this guy in my office was trying to find some indication of where we're hiding out. He specifically asked Karen where 'we' were."

"So he could get the disk."

"Maybe. Or maybe he was looking for you."

She tried to reason this out. The guy was wearing a mask, so he was afraid someone would recognize him. It wasn't Detry. Detry had been at a restaurant with Chloe, two of her bridesmaids, two of the groomsmen, Angie and Boone from noon till two. If Detry wanted to hire someone to kill or kidnap her, he knew right where she was.

She had to face it. She still believed Detry was evil—that hadn't changed—but he was not tied in to the guys in the Mustang or the break-in at Boone's office.

Mercy.

"If it makes you feel any better, only Jack knows we're here, and he won't tell anyone, not even your boss. We're as good as in hiding."

She nodded slowly. Her sister and her mother were safe, then.

Processing all this was difficult. "If it's not Detry who wants me dead, then it's probably someone tied in with Cliff's death, right?"

He nodded.

Her irritation spiked off the meter. She couldn't focus on her sister with this going on. "This has gone too far. We need to go back to Copper City and draw this guy out."

"No." Boone's face was pure opposition.

"You wouldn't spend five minutes in hiding if you thought you could catch someone trying to murder you. So why aren't you giving me the same freedom?"

"The freedom to run away from your past again?"

"I'm not running away," she insisted, pulling the chain strap on her white leather purse higher on her shoulder. She took a deep breath to calm down and lowered her voice. "I've decided not to confront Mom. I have enough to deal with right now between Detry and whoever wants to put me out of my misery. I doubt if talking to her would change anything anyway."

"You're afraid of what she might say." He took her hand.

She tried hard to level Boone with her cop stare. "You're being almost insistent about my talking to Mom, and I don't understand why it matters to you so much."

"I saw how she is with you at dinner the first night. She's so detached from you, but not from Chloe. There has to be a reason."

"She resented having a second child." At least, that was what she'd been telling herself for years. Angie felt her chin quiver and clamped her teeth together tightly for a second. "Again, I don't understand why you care."

Inside the bridal shower, a burst of applause diverted them, but only for a second. Undaunted, Boone stared right back at her. "Because you matter to me. Because if you talk to her and find out why she's like she is, maybe you'll change your mind about children—"

"And you and I can finally get married and have the family you always wanted?"

"Would that be so bad?" he asked. His blue eyes held such hope.

"No, if you'd just told me that was your agenda in getting me away from the investigation in Copper City all along." The corners of her mouth turned downward. "And what happens if I talk to Madeleine and find out there's no particular reason for the way she was, and I'm right back where I started, with the same doubts as always? Would I still be so wonderful to you?"

"It won't be that way."

"Oh, Boone," she said, regret thick in her voice. "You can't manipulate the people in your life until they're exactly the way you want them to be. Why can't you just love me for who I am, instead of what I can give you?"

Boone's heart squeezed painfully. He was failing at words again. This was his mistake. She'd made it clear from the beginning she hadn't wanted this kind of connection between them. He should have listened instead of hoping for something that was never going to be.

"I'm sorry. I shouldn't have said anything—it wasn't my place to reopen old wounds. I overstepped the boundaries between us."

"Yes, you did."

"From this point on, we'll keep things light until we catch whoever it is who is after you, and then we'll go our separate ways."

She didn't open her mouth to agree with him. That left Boone even more confused. Instead, she sighed and turned her attention to the far end of the still-empty hall, where the exit sign was.

"What are you looking for?" he asked.

She looked at him and shook her head. "The cavalry. I just hope you and I aren't it. If we are, we're doomed."

He didn't smile. That was fine, she wasn't smiling, either.

Standing, she headed toward the nearby ladies' room. She planned to stay in there until he gave up watching for her. Or until the new break in her heart healed.

Yeah, like she didn't already have a Humpty Dumpty heart.

The ladies' room was more like a lounge, almost six times the size of the one in Ida's biker bar, with two sections. The far one held stalls and a second exit. She chose the first section with its handful of cushioned chairs at the far end, and basins and brightly lit mirrors lining the long walls. Next to the chairs were tissues and a basket of red-foil-wrapped chocolates, and she grabbed one of each as she sank down on a chair, her silk skirt swishing around her.

She tore off the wrapper and stuck the candy into her mouth with no illusions it would help. Mellowing out would take the whole basket.

The argument she and Boone had just had was for the best. Clearing the air and all that. What did it matter, really, that she still had feelings for him? He wasn't going to change. All that mattered was that she save her sister's life, and that she was doing what God wanted her to.

She was so glad she wasn't a crier.

She heard the squeak of a stall door—strange in such a fancy place. Other people were in here after all. She needed to get her act together. Rising, she threw away the chocolate wrapper, checked her teeth and turned.

Ida peeked around the corner.

"I knew if I just hid long enough, one or the other of you would come in here," Ida said. "Your sister, not the eye magnet, I mean."

"You came!" Angie hurried to join her. She started to throw her arms around Ida, but backed off when she saw the nervous look on the other woman's face.

"Let's just talk to your sister and let me get out of here. Because if someone thinks I'm the cleaning service from the way

I'm not dressed like you and hands me a mop and bucket, I'd have to hit them."

A breathy chuckle escaped Angie's lips. "I wouldn't let them, don't worry. I'll go get Chloe."

Before she could, the door opposite them opened, and Chloe peeked inside. "You *are* in here!" she said, her face brightening when she saw Angie. "I was wondering where you went off to and Boone told me to check here. The party's almost over."

"I'll say," Ida muttered. Angie shushed her as Chloe joined them. She said a short prayer under her breath and introduced Ida as her friend. True to her nature, Ida plunged right into the deep end.

"You don't know me. But I came to tell you something about your fiancé. It's a matter of life and death."

Chloe's eyes blinked in surprise.

"I knew your Warren Detry by a different name a long time ago. He dated my daughter, then murdered her. I don't know why. He set fire to the house she was in, and a couple of others, to cover it up. You have to believe me, he's very dangerous."

Angie watched Chloe closely. Caught off-guard by Ida, Chloe stared, her eyes huge. She looked at both Ida and Angie in turn, her eyes narrowing in suspicion.

"Did my sister make you come talk to me?"

Ida clamped her hands on her jeans-clad hips, making her silver bracelets clink. "No one makes me do anything, young lady. I'm here only because I am afraid for you. I don't want you to end up in a grave like my little girl did."

"I'm sorry that happened." Chloe's expression softened, and she turned to Angie. "You still believe Warren could kill someone? Anyone?"

"Yes. We found the missing murder weapon from his wife's gun collection a couple days ago, Chloe, and it has Warren's prints on it."

"I know about that weapon from the newspaper reports about your testimony," Chloe said slowly, sounding as if she was trying hard to be patient. "Warren told me he never noticed whether the gun was out of its case or not before you arrested him and he went to prison to await trial. When Boone told him what the murder weapon supposedly was, he admitted it was part of his wife's collection, but then he found out that his home had been broken into and items stolen very soon after he was arrested. He told Boone, but Boone said there was no police report about the weapon."

Angie frowned. She hadn't heard about a burglary. Not even Boone had mentioned it in the trial. Had Cliff Haggis buried the police report about it, too? None of that made sense.

"He also said he often showed it to friends, and even shot it once. So I am not concerned about his prints on that gun." She swung her head back to Ida. "Do you have proof Warren murdered your daughter?"

Ida spread her hands out, showing empty palms. "No. But it couldn't have been anyone else."

"Why didn't the police department go after him?"

"He disappeared that night and never returned."

"Why do you think her killer is my Warren?"

"He—" Ida started, but then her eyes flew to Angie, and abruptly, to Angie's shock, she stopped speaking with a shake of her head.

Frustration boiled in Angie. "Ida, whatever it is, tell her."

"I can't," Ida said, real regret in her eyes. "I'm sorry, Angie. I knew she wouldn't believe me without proof. Nobody would."

Angie's heart sank. Ida was hiding something she didn't want her or Chloe to know, maybe even the key to the whole mess about the man now calling himself Detry. But she couldn't prove that any more than she could prove Detry really murdered his wife, or Ida's daughter, for that matter.

Crushed, Chloe took a shuddering breath as she turned to Angie. "I can't believe you convinced this poor lady to tell me some tale about Warren and her daughter."

"It's not a tale, it's a fact," Ida insisted. "Warren Detry is Wayne Donaldson, and he did murder my daughter and then he hired a thug to murder your sister and take me out, too."

Angie froze, her heart falling. She couldn't let that go—it wouldn't be right. "Actually, it turns out the thug was hired by someone else, Ida. We don't know who yet."

Ida, startled, stared at her. Chloe looked incredulous.

"He hurt you already, Chloe," Angie said, trying to recover. "He *bruised* you. Don't you sense the capability for extreme anger in him at all?"

Chloe's head shook back and forth, hard. "No. I don't. That was an *accident.*" Tears formed in her eyes as she stared at Angie. "I really thought you had forgiven me for the past. Is this why you came home? To hurt me again by taking away another fiancé? To take revenge for me being selfish growing up? Well, this time you failed."

"I just want to keep you alive," Angie protested.

"I'm marrying Warren." Her sister's hand shook as she raised it in emphasis. "And I don't want a big scene at home with Mom finding out about this and throwing you out again. I don't want that memory attached to the happiest day of my life. I'm not even going to tell her about this. You can attend the rehearsal dinner Friday and the wedding on Saturday if you stay in the background, but until then, it might be best if you made an excuse and left." Brushing past Angie, Chloe left the lounge.

Angie pulled in a huge breath as she leaned back against a stall door and covered her face with her hands.

"You aren't crying, are you?" Ida asked, worry in her voice.

"I want to." She was close, too. She rubbed her face to push back the tears and let her hands drop to her sides, shaking them out. "Boy, do I want to. I was so wrong about Detry. I thought I was hearing God, and I was only listening to myself. I totally blew it."

Ida's shoulders went straight, and her chin went up in a no-nonsense stance. "Dramatics might work with the eye magnet, but not with me. I invented dramatics. Your sister's not married yet. Buck up. God doesn't necessarily need you to do all His work, you know."

The verbal shaking helped. She had to get a grip and remember God was in control. She was getting to be like Boone, thinking it all depended on him, and that wasn't good.

Ida glanced down at her steel-gray, leather-banded watch. "I'd better get back to the car before the boys get worried. But first I gotta know. You're getting the hero and moving out of that house, right? Bright Eyes there—" she thrust a thumb over her shoulder toward the door to indicate Chloe "—is going to run right to Detry for comfort and tell him how bad you are, if I know human nature—and I do. Her fiancé might not have sent those other guys, but he does have a killer temper, and he ain't gonna like us crossing him like this. You gotta run and get hidden, like I am."

"Do you think Detry will come after you?"

Ida's eyes were steady as she gazed at her. "I think he's capable of anything when he's angry."

Wasn't that what she wanted, for Detry to show his true colors? Another idea began to form in Angie's mind. She wasn't going to find proof, she realized that now, but if she could lure him into a trap and he tried to kill her, that would be enough to stop the wedding and put him away.

She'd have to think about that. Pray about that, she corrected. She was trusting God to stop her if she was making the wrong decision.

Before she did anything about Detry, though, she wanted to

go to Cliff's funeral and say her final goodbyes. He might have made a big mistake with the evidence and hurt her reputation, but he'd been sorry and tried to make amends. He was easy to forgive.

"I see your gears turning, Angie," Ida said.

"I could use a favor, but I've got to warn you—Boone will more than likely be furious at you if you help me."

Ida grinned at her. "The day I can't handle a man, I'm selling the bar and going to a rest home."

"Okay, then." She nodded, resolute. "I need a place to stay tonight and a ride to a funeral tomorrow, and then maybe a ride back to my mother's house afterward. I'm not sure about the last part. I haven't totally formed my new plan yet."

"Tell you what. How about I just loan you a car tomorrow morning?"

"That'll work, too." She caught Ida's arm. "Thanks for trying with Chloe, Ida. I really appreciate it."

The woman's eyes went all soft again. "Yeah. I had to do it."

"That's what makes it even more special, Ida. You didn't have to."

Ida gave her a sharp nod. "Yeah, hon, I did." With that, the older woman gave a dismissive wave of her hand. "Now, how are we gonna get past the eye magnet?"

"I'll just tell him I'm going with you. There's not a lot he can do about it."

"Oh, boy. I'd rather face a drunk biker," Ida said.

"Boone isn't that bad." The fact that she automatically defended him annoyed her, but she let it rest, since it was the truth.

"Not bad, Angie. Sad. I don't think he's gonna want to let loose of you."

She wouldn't be surprised at that, but he had no choice. She had a life or death mission, and if she told him her next step to achieving it, he would stand in her way. She couldn't let him do that.

* * *

Despite the hall filling with women, Boone hadn't moved from his spot against the beige wall. As Angie and Ida grew closer, he drew himself up to his full height, his narrowed eyes speaking volumes. Boone was not happy. He must have seen Chloe crying and figured out that Angie had finally confronted her.

"You. Me. Outside," he said.

"That'll work." They needed to talk, and there were too many people in the hall.

She didn't speak until they reached Boone's Mercedes. Ida's gaze kept moving anxiously around them, and she spoke first.

"Since you two are going to talk, I'm going to wait by the van. I don't like being out in the open."

Much as Angie wanted to talk to Boone, she didn't want Ida to be afraid. "Detry went to work this afternoon. You're in no danger."

"Ha!" Ida said bluntly. "I'll wait for you."

Angie nodded. Her eyes followed Ida the few dozen feet through late model cars to a sturdy-looking, dusty and scratched white van. Micah waved from the window, and Angie lifted her hand in reply. She turned back to Boone.

"I guess you could tell. I'm going to stay with Ida tonight."

"You're running away again," Boone told her.

Ida was right. He did sound sad. "I'm trying to stay safe. I confronted Chloe about Detry with Ida as a backup. Let's just say Chloe wasn't happy, and I don't think Detry will be, either."

"Oh, Angel." He shook his head with an unbelieving look in his eyes. "I'm assuming Ida does have a connection to Detry that isn't good, and she finally told you? And if she did, why didn't you discuss it with Jack?"

Why didn't you discuss it with me? he meant.

"I didn't tell *you*," she said pointedly, "because you wouldn't believe it was him." Just to prove it to herself, she filled Boone in on Wayne Donaldson's background. "The biggest problem is she has no proof Donaldson is Detry."

"I talked to two people who went to high school with Warren Detry," Boone said. "Their description of him fit, right down to a scar on his leg he got when he was hit by a car when he was twelve. I really don't think Ida has the right man. But we could look into it."

He was humoring her, Angie could tell. "Donaldson might have given himself a scar before or after he assumed Warren Detry's identity."

"You're grasping for anything that will prove you're right that he's a murderer. Why?"

"His eyes." There, now he knew. "The way he looked at me when we first met. Ida saw it, too. I get this feeling when I look at him, Boone, that he's done something horrible."

"Angie." His voice was edged with frustration and maybe a bit of anger. "You sure this doesn't have something to do with an unwillingness to forgive your mother and Chloe for the way they treated you? A vengeance of sorts?"

"I wouldn't do that." Angie worked her bottom lip. "I can't believe you think I would."

"I don't know what to think."

Her fragile, barely-there hopes for the two of them shattered like the thin ice their relationship had been on for the past year.

"Did Jack find out who the other person was on the footage yet?" she asked, needing to know that before she left with Ida. At the rate she and Boone were going, she didn't know if she'd ever see him again.

She knew about the two men, yet she'd held that back from him, too. Boone's irritation grew.

"The investigation is ongoing. I can't tell you."

"I'm a cop."

"You're the victim."

Boone had a reason for being close-mouthed. Jack *had* called while Angie was trying to ruin Chloe's wedding in the ladies' lounge. Detry was in the cemetery footage, visiting his wife's grave and praying. But Angie knew that. Ida would have recognized Detry and told her.

The second man had come later, in the dead of night. Jack had known him immediately. Just like Boone and Angie, the man had used a metal detector to search around Laurie's grave, but not around the flowers, so he'd found nothing.

Armed with the identity of the second man on the disk, Jack had finally been able to match the prints on the murder weapon. It had taken awhile, because getting a cop's fingerprints from his file took a court order.

The cop was Chief Roy Gregg.

With that ammunition, Jack had gotten Thatcher to confess in minutes that Gregg had hired him to murder Angie and Ida, but he wouldn't say why. Chief Gregg had probably also been behind Cliff Haggis's murder, but Jack was still gathering information on that.

Boone gazed down at the blond woman in front of him. She was brave and wanted justice, and Boone couldn't chance she would try going after Gregg herself, so he wasn't about to tell her about the chief. Jack figured they would have him captured by tomorrow. Boone planned to make sure of that. Until then, Boone had to protect her from herself.

Angie's teeth gritted. She was miffed, but he couldn't help that.

"I'll be able to tell you more tomorrow," he said. "If you want to go with Ida, fine. Just *please* stay there where you'll be safe until I call. Do not go to that funeral. And do not mess with Detry until we have a chance to look into Ida's story."

"Why would you do that? Your mind is made up."

"Because if we clear Detry, maybe you'll finally focus on yourself. If you would just trust me, everything will work out for the best."

He cared about her, and she was beginning to understand that caring, in Boone's eyes, was real love. He wanted to protect her, and see her happy, with a family. She wished she could stay put at Ida's and let Boone be the hero. To just do things his way. Trouble was, he didn't think her sister was in danger. She did. Tomorrow, she was going to try trapping Detry and proving he was capable of violence so her sister could finally see the man as he really was. And Boone was going to hate that. Oh, yeah.

"And if I don't do what you want?" To do so would mean to give up on trying to help Chloe, and she didn't think that was what God wanted. She'd be putting Boone's wishes over God's. It would also mean forgiving her mother, no matter what her reasons were for her emotional neglect, and trying to not worry about being a good mother herself. What if she couldn't do either?

"Angie, I don't want to lose you," Boone said.

"I think it's too late for that."

She would remember the sadness in his eyes forever.

"Is it safe for me to go back and get my things from Madeleine's?" Boone asked.

"You're their hero, Boone. You saved the groom. I don't see why not. Actually, I'm going to ask Micah to stop by there myself so I can pick up my clothes. They'll both be happy to see me go. Chloe said she wouldn't tell Madeleine I was trying to break them up, but I think Chloe'd be happiest if she never had to speak to me again."

"Oh, Angel." He gave a sad shake of his head. "I'll never stop talking to you, no matter how mad you make me."

Her lips quivered. "I'm grateful for that."

With sadness in his eyes, he offered her a half smile. "I'm going to miss you."

"I'm going to miss you, too," she whispered. Impulsively, because after tomorrow and her confrontation with Detry, she knew it would be over between them, she threw her arms around Boone's neck and kissed him. He kissed her back. She almost changed her mind about trapping Detry. All she had to do was hide out with Ida and let Boone handle everything.

But then who would save her sister? Boone didn't *believe*. Not in Detry's guilt, in her or in God.

Real life and love—boy, they hurt.

She pressed her fingers to his lips, then hurried off to Ida's van. At least she knew Boone would be safe when she went to trap the man who was playing death games with her sister's life.

Boone felt his heart leaving with her. He wanted, desperately, to keep her with him, close to him, and not just to keep her secure, either. He wished he could go after her, but he needed to be there when Jack arrested Chief Gregg. To make sure the man was in prison and couldn't hurt Angie, ever.

Always, his sense of duty came before something he desired about as much as his life itself. If only he could do what she wanted him to, be who she wanted him to be, but he couldn't. All he could do was make sure no one ever tried to kill her again.

But it hurt.

TEN

If Angie was alive when he caught up to her, Boone thought, first he was going to kiss her, then he was going to throttle her. She had left Ida's. Whether purposely or because she thought he was another threat, Boone didn't know, but she'd also dodged the bodyguard he'd hired. Boone had sent him to Cliff Haggis's funeral, her most likely destination. He wanted to go after her himself, but he was needed where he was to capture Chief Gregg.

Boone had called Gregg the night before and offered him the disk and a chance to get out of town in exchange for not going near Angie again. Gregg hadn't confessed, nor admitted guilt, just promised to meet him at the end of the access road at the rear of the Last Stop Cemetery, where there were no cameras. And where Jack and his men, hidden in various spots for now, would arrest him.

Boone paced the length of the access road from the boundary fence to Sonny's van, stopped near the body-shop owner, and turned again.

"Look, I'm wearing this vest like you asked," Sonny told him. "Quit worrying about me so much."

Boone stopped short, looked at his burly friend made even larger by the bulletproof vest and broke out into a short but heartfelt, grin. "Funny."

"Comedy was my first love. Before auto-body repair." Sonny grinned back. "You keep being distracted like this, that cop's gonna get the best of you."

"I'm worried about Angie."

Sonny shrugged his shoulders. "What's to worry? You got a bodyguard going to protect her, no?"

"Yeah, but—"

"But it's not you."

Could everyone see right through him like that?

"Hey, I know the feeling, being worried about a woman. I'm married, too."

"I'm not married."

"Uh, okay," Sonny said, as though he might as well be.

So Sonny would know he wasn't angry with him, Boone gave his arm a tap with his knuckles. "Thanks for backing me up today."

"Hey, you defended me for free and then gave me the money to open my own garage after I lost everything I had sitting in prison before the trial. Like I'm not gonna help you? Get real."

He, Sonny, Jack and his deputies were all wired, so Jack, in the back of the van, was picking up the whole conversation, and probably enjoying himself immensely.

Jack always did.

Boone gazed out to two tall grave markers on either side of them, behind which a couple more officers were waiting. A Closed sign hung from the cemetery gates, but he'd told Gregg to ignore it. Everything was set.

Except where was Gregg?

Angie settled in her regular pew in the church she'd considered her own since Cliff and his wife, Marta, had first invited her there. Immediately, some of the parishioners, people she considered family, waved at her or came over to offer a somber hello and hug her, and she didn't feel so alone anymore. She still felt sad. Cliff was gone. Chloe hated her. And worst of all, she had no chance of getting back together with Boone.

Life just didn't get any easier.

The organ music started and people settled down. She gazed around the medium-sized sanctuary, and then up at a window with the red, blue and purple stained glass. The sun shone through, lighting up the windows magnificently. Despite the pain in her heart, she found peace and warmth here. She wished Boone could, too.

Bowing her head during the opening prayer, she prayed fervently for Boone, and for Cliff's wife. She lifted her head when she felt fingers on her wrist, which was at her side draped over her purse. Boone? Opening her eyes, smiling, she turned in her seat to greet him—and her words froze on her lips.

It was Warren Detry.

His jaw was like stone, his eyes narrowed and razor sharp and his fingers felt like an alligator had clamped down on her wrist. He didn't say a word. Her heart thumped and raced, but she stared back. Finally, he released her and turned to face the front as a soloist started to sing.

Chloe had spoken to him about what she'd said, and he was furious—that was obvious. His confronting her and trying something was exactly what she'd wanted, but on her own terms, not his. He had the advantage. That wasn't good.

She glanced around—no free seats. Considered leaving—Detry might follow, and he'd still have the advantage. She moved her purse to the other side of her and undid the button on her suit jacket, one step closer to her duty weapon. She felt better—not that she'd draw it in here.

Her ideas ran out. But not her desire to bring Detry down before he could hurt her sister—oh, no. Somehow, she would find a way.

* * *

"He's not coming," Boone said into his mike. "Abort."

The back door of the van crunched open, and Jack swung out and strode over to them, flipping his cell phone closed. The other deputies left their posts and walked toward the van, their ride out of the cemetery.

"No word at all from the man stationed outside the cemetery," Jack told Boone. "Gregg's tail is still by his house. He must have evaded him somehow." His eyes swept the street beyond the cemetery boundary. "He could have sent someone for a drive by here, caught us setting up and figured it was a trap."

Boone's phone rang. Expecting Gregg, Boone felt his heart race when he saw the number for the bodyguard. He was at the jail, arrested for loitering outside the church by Chief Gregg. Boone told him to hang tight and hung up.

"Gregg's at the funeral. He's going after Angie."

They all ran for the van. In seconds, Sonny revved up the motor, and once the back door slammed shut with all the deputies inside, Sonny gunned it. "Where to?"

"Victory Community Church," Boone said. "Hurry."

Sonny nodded grimly. "Don't worry, no chance of him getting away this time. We got an army."

The cavalry, Boone thought, remembering his conversation with Angie. He yanked on his seat belt as Sonny exited the cemetery on two wheels. She'd love that.

If Gregg didn't kill her first.

Detry's eyes said he wanted to kill her—this time Angie had no doubts at all. He'd grabbed her wrist again just as Cliff's widow left through the rear entrance, and was now pulling her into the aisle. She hung back, but he sent her another look, and she feared he might actually hurt someone else.

She couldn't make a defensive move with so many people right there who could get hurt, including children. He pulled her out the door, down the brick steps and through the dispersing people around to the side of the church. No one stood back there between the church and the parsonage, but people were still within shouting distance in front.

He stood before her, his eyes boring into hers. He was waiting, and for the life of her, she didn't know for what. She put a lock on her fear. It was time to end this.

"Angry with me for clueing Chloe in on your past, Detry?"

"All I ever wanted," he said slowly, "was to have a family of my own. Surely you understand that, after all you've been through."

Chloe must have told him about her broken engagement to Boone. That she'd never had much of a real family and held no prospects of getting one anytime soon was not something she wanted to chat about with a murderer.

"Talk about what's really going on here," she ordered, "not about something you don't have any knowledge of."

A puzzled look swept over his face. He released his hold on her wrist and backed up, frowning at her as though he was trying to figure out something.

What on earth? Angie stepped back. She resisted the urge to rub her wrist, not wanting to give him the satisfaction.

"You don't know, do you?" he asked.

"Yeah, I know. That you're really Wayne Donaldson, and you murdered your girlfriend and set fire to her house and half of Colleyville."

He waited another moment, then his whole face changed. His smile was like an ice cube going up and down her spine.

"You can't prove I did any of that," he said.

"You also murdered Laurie Detry."

The angry evil that had been haunting her all along fired up again in his eyes. Sudden. Frightening. "I did not kill Laurie. I loved her."

"Why did you come here?" she asked, ignoring his protests of innocence. Her voice might be authoritative, but inside she was a little girl again, a trembling mass of nerves.

It was his eyes. They reminded her of something, someone, but she couldn't remember what. She needed to.

He laughed, an eerie chuckle that played again and again in the back of her mind. "I came for the same reason you did—to pay my respects to the man who helped free me."

The man who helped free me. To anyone who didn't know about the buried evidence, Detry's words were innocent enough, just describing Cliff's testimony at the trial. But to her, his words held a whole other meaning.

"Helped free you and sacrificed his integrity to do so," she said. "Did you kill him to shut him up?"

"Angie, Angie…" Detry shook his head slowly. "I did not kill Cliff Haggis. And you need to accept the things you cannot change. Anger built up inside you can only bring you and everyone around you to great harm. I'm sure you don't want to see that happen."

"I plan on making certain it doesn't." Every muscle within her tensed. She had anger in her, all right—righteous anger. She planned on explaining the difference to him the minute she slapped the cuffs on him.

"You asked me why I was here?" His smile was gone. "Your sister told me you already broke up her first engagement. If you're thinking to do that again, you might not have a family left." He paused, letting that sink in. "You do know how important family is, don't you, Angie? How much family can love and protect you? Oh, I almost forgot. You gave that all up, didn't you?"

He should have stuck a blade into her heart—that would have

hurt less. She hadn't given up the warm cocoon of family—
she'd never had it in the first place. His words reminded her of
everything she'd never had, her father's presence, her mother's
love, her sister's real friendship. And of everything she'd lost
because of Detry…like her chance at true happiness with Boone.

The words tumbled out before she could think, or pray,
about them.

"Before I just wanted to keep you from marrying Chloe. Now
I'm making it my life's mission to make sure you rot in prison
for what you did. You'll never have Chloe, and you'll never have
any children."

All the mocking left Detry's eyes. They darkened to the color
of his black heart, then evil burned in them like that night she'd
first seen him.

She didn't understand how or why, but she knew to prepare for
what was coming. She moved her foot backward, shifted her weight.

He raised his fist in the air.

She kicked his kneecap. The impact jarred her shin, which only
made her angrier. She grabbed his arm to twist it behind his back,
felt him resist. Hooking his ankle, she threw him off-balance to
the ground, facedown, and put her knee into the small of his back.

She vaguely registered a voice yelling in the distance when
she spoke.

"You're under arrest for attempted assault on a police officer."
Her heart boomed in her chest, her hair bounced and blocked her
vision and Detry twisted. Anger driving her on, she drew her gun.

Detry uttered a name no woman should be called.

It didn't matter. She had him. He was going to go to jail for
attempted assault on a police officer, and stay there when they
found proof he'd murdered Ida's daughter, and her sister was
going to be safe. She had him.

She finally had him.

"Let him go, Officer Delitano."

She peered upward through a veil of hair. Her boss. Chief Gregg stood above her in jeans and a casual blue denim shirt, wearing his hip holster, his weapon drawn.

"Why aren't you in uniform?" she asked. Since learning Cliff had been murdered, many of her coworkers had worn theirs to honor him. She hadn't only because it had gotten wrinkled in her traveling and Ida didn't own an iron. But the chief, not in uniform? Inconceivable.

Gregg shot her the same sort of puzzled look Detry had given her before, as if she should know something she didn't. She felt out of the loop. He waved his gun. "Get up."

Sighing with relief that she had help taking Detry in, she pushed off of his back. That was when she remembered she'd last seen her cuffs on Thatcher, at Ida's bar.

"Can I borrow your cuffs?" she asked Chief Gregg. She could see a pair on his belt.

"What happened?" Chief Gregg demanded without answering her question. She didn't even wince at his tone—she was used to it.

"He raised his hand to punch me, and I arrested him for attempted assault."

"Mr. Detry?" Gregg kept his gun in one hand, but bent enough to assist Detry to his feet and give him a courteous nod. Angie frowned. Another backlash of that day in court when Boone had made her look like a fool—the chief had ceased to trust her judgment as a cop, too.

Detry brushed the grass off his suit. "Your officer arrested me for warning her not to interfere with my upcoming plans to marry her sister."

Confusion flooded the chief's face. "You're marrying the officer's sister?"

"This Saturday." Detry nodded slowly, his face full of satisfaction.

Angie shook her head. "Don't count on it, Donaldson."

"See?" Detry said to the chief. "Your officer is very confused."

"He was Wayne Donaldson of Colleyville, and he changed his name when he ran from arson and murder there," she explained crisply. Apart from it being Ida's belief, she didn't know why she was willing to stake her career on it, but she was.

The chief regarded her with a long look. "You thought to stop the wedding by arresting him?"

"He made a threat against my sister's and mother's lives. Then he raised his fist when I told him I—"

"No, I did not," Detry interrupted. "I would never ruin my relationship with my fiancée by striking her sister, no matter how irritated I might get over something she says."

Chief Gregg asked, "Did anyone hear what was said? See any of it?"

For the first time, Angie gazed toward the street. There were a few people standing there, gesturing at them, probably because of the weapons they both still held.

"I don't know."

"I'll ask," Gregg said impatiently. "Wait here."

As soon as he was out of earshot, Detry turned to her. "Chloe's going to hate you. Just admit you did wrong, and we won't mention this episode to her."

"Give it up, Detry. You're under arrest."

"It was this pigheadedness that got you in trouble before, Officer."

She moved her position so she could both cover him and watch the chief. Gregg was shaking his head and making the crowd disperse. When no one was left, he turned and strode back to them, his face grim.

"No one saw anything." Turning to Detry, he said simply, "You're free to go, with my apology on behalf of the Copper City PD."

She couldn't believe this. "He was going to assault me."

"Holster your weapon, Delitano. It's his word against yours."

She had to obey the chief, even though it was against her better judgment and galled her to have Detry see her brought down a peg.

"I'll admit I was angry with you after the trial for insisting I murdered my beloved wife." Detry smiled at Angie as though he were being the most gracious man on earth. "I even sent you that e-mail, and I apologize. But I no longer harbor hard feelings against you. After all, you're going to be *family.*"

The way he said the last word made Angie's skin crawl. She gritted her teeth to keep from saying something in front of Chief Gregg. She didn't have anything left but her job. She wanted to keep it.

Detry turned and walked swiftly toward the street. He was going free again. Her stomach churned. She bit down on her tongue to make sure she didn't use it to say something stupid to Gregg, and turned to walk away herself.

"I didn't dismiss you."

Angie froze. Her cell phone rang, but she ignored it.

The chief joined her where she was. "Officer Delitano, I'm inclined to believe Mr. Detry's version of this. His reason for not hitting you was more sound than what you claimed happened. I believe your antagonism toward him because of his engagement to your sister caused you to jump the gun."

"So you're saying I'm either a liar or an idiot, who can't tell when she's being attacked."

"You have a background of being mistaken. I run a tight ship and need officers who can do their jobs. You need to give me your weapon and your badge immediately. You're suspended, pending a hearing. I expect you're finished as a cop."

Blood pounded in her ears. First Boone, then her mother and Chloe, gone. She wasn't letting her job go now without a fight, or she would have nothing left.

Seething inside, she almost opened her mouth to let Gregg know how wrong he was. She hadn't been mistaken about the murder weapon. But she couldn't tell him where it was, or that the sheriff's department was investigating everything about that, and Cliff's murder. He might interfere in some way, and she didn't want that.

She wanted Cliff's killer caught.

"I'm protesting this to my delegate," she said, referring to the union rep they were all assigned.

"I want your duty weapon and badge now, Officer Delitano, before you bring more shame down on my department."

Opening her purse, she took out her badge and slapped it into his palm. He put it in his pants pocket. "Your weapon?"

Grudgingly, she removed it from her holster and handed it to him. He stuck it in the rear of his waistband.

"I'll escort you to your vehicle, just in case Mr. Detry hasn't left the premises yet."

"I don't think that's necessary," she told him, and headed in that direction, seething. She couldn't go after Detry again—he could now claim police harassment and Chief Gregg would back him up. She couldn't save her sister if she got arrested. It was over. She'd lost.

Angry didn't begin to describe how she was feeling. Only she wasn't certain whom she was angry at: Detry for getting to her before she got to him, Chief Gregg for messing up her arrest, Boone for indirectly causing Chief Gregg to doubt her, or God for not letting her save her sister.

It didn't look like He planned to, either.

I still believe, she muttered under her breath as she reached the inexpensive import Ida had lent her. She really truly did. God existed, but maybe Boone's idea about Him was more right than what she'd learned about Him from Cliff. Maybe all the prayer in the world didn't help, and God wasn't guiding her.

Maybe God did sit back and let them all do what they wanted with their free will, and if you believed in God and did the right thing, at the end, He would be pleased and you'd end up in Heaven. Sometimes doing the right thing would work, and sometimes it would get you killed.

"Lord, I don't want it to be like that," she whispered. She wanted to know God cared about her, just like the Bible said. That He was watching out for her sister. "Show me she'll be safe?"

"God's not going to help you now."

She jolted as if she'd stuck her finger into a light socket. Before she could turn, Chief Gregg pushed her against the car, grabbed her arm and twisted it around sharply, sending a stabbing pain up her forearm. A bolt of fear jammed through her stomach. The cool steel of his cuffs snapped on her wrist.

He was arresting her for Detry? Something wasn't right.

Her fight instinct kicked in. She stepped backward on his instep. He grunted and grabbed for her other arm. Desperate, she flailed it to attract attention and yelled for help.

It worked. Pastor Kaminski, on the church steps, started toward them.

"Chief Roy Gregg, Copper City Police Department," Gregg called out, flashing his badge in the air and then pocketing it. "Don't interfere, Pastor."

"Pastor," she screamed, "call Jack Callahan, Sheriff's—"

"Shut up," Gregg warned darkly. He finished cuffing her in seconds, then turned her around, so she couldn't see if Pastor

Kaminski stopped or not. His muscular forearm held her against the car as he patted the two sides of her jacket. Her keys jangled, and he lifted them from her pocket.

Yanking her around, he unlocked the car, pushed her into the passenger's seat and slammed the door. She tried to maneuver and open the door, but he'd locked it. She finally managed to flip that up, but he was in the driver's seat, saw what she was doing and jerked her around. He took a few seconds to search her purse, then threw it to the floor. Cursing, he pulled out into the thinning funeral traffic.

Then she understood. This wasn't about Warren Detry at all.

This was about Thatcher shooting at her head.

This was about the unknown man on the cemetery footage.

This was about Chief Gregg himself.

She bowed her head and started to pray.

"Praying won't help, Angie. You should have listened to the warning note I left on your car." Gregg's glance was cold. "No one is going to help you now. Not your boyfriend, not the sheriff's department and not God."

"How do you know?" Angie asked. Her skin went clammy and her arms numbed. She knew God was right there with her, but still sweat broke out on her forehead. She should get angry enough to fight Gregg if she got a chance, but right then, she just felt sick.

"God doesn't exist," the chief told her.

"He does." She suddenly realized why she felt sick. God didn't want her to fight him. He wanted her to tell him about Jesus, who could save him.

Not that, Lord. Please, not that. She was supposed to witness to the person who wanted her dead?

She wasn't in that good of a mood.

A drop of sweat rolled into her eyes. She gave in. "God exists, and he had a plan for all of us. It involves Jesus—"

"Didn't I tell you to shut up before? I know all about that stuff. Jesus died to save us. We believe, and we get eternal life and all that. Yeah, right. You talk too much. Always did. You shouldn't have talked to Cliff. You shouldn't have talked in court. You shouldn't be talking about God now while I have two guns on me." He winced. "Forget it. I'm too far gone."

"Nobody is too far gone that they can't be forgiven."

"Oh, yeah? I had your husband, Tony, killed." Gregg's face was harsh as he glanced at her. "Still think that?"

Blood drummed in her ears. All this time working for Gregg—and he'd killed Tony? "Why?"

"I shouldn't have told you that." He cursed. "Now I'll have to kill you."

It was a popular joke, but Angie knew he wasn't kidding. "Why did you kill Tony?"

"He was distributing for me, and he said he got ripped off for a hundred bucks' worth of drugs. He lied. I had him killed as an example to others working for me. Can you forgive that? Can God?"

She took deep breaths, one after the other. She was supposed to answer, but she couldn't. *He killed Tony.*

"I thought so," he said, nodding.

She closed her eyes. The morning he was killed, Tony had come into the bank where she worked with a gold, heart-shaped locket for her. Had that been where Gregg's missing hundred went? On it was engraved *"You Are Loved."* For Valentine's Day. It was the first time anyone had ever loved her like that, flawed as Tony had been.

As flawed as she was then, and was now.

She wanted that love again. She wanted Boone.

"Now tell me, and don't take a year drumming up some story. Where's the evidence?"

"I gave the murder weapon to the sheriff's department. You had to have figured I would."

He punched her arm with his fist, hard and fast. Hot tears of pain filled her eyes.

"Don't mess with me. I don't care about that gun. I was having an affair with Laurie Detry since the toy drive. She showed me her antique gun. Of course my prints would be on it. No proof."

Angie's arm hurt, and she was mad. Red-hot, muscles-tight mad. But he'd just told her something important. She couldn't lose her temper. She had to concentrate.

He knew Laurie Detry. His prints were on the gun. "You want the disk, then?" she said, swallowing her pride and trying to sound meek. "With the cemetery footage with you on it?" The last was a guess.

"No, Officer Delitano, not the cemetery footage," he said in a tone that implied she was stupid. "I have a good excuse for being on that, too. I found out Cliff hid the murder weapon and was looking for it so I could clear your name." He lifted his arm as if he would hit her again, and she moved back as far as she could.

"The papers!" His yell filled the tiny car. "I want the papers you took. Santiago told me you were in the office and almost walked out with a file. I figure you had to have taken the papers. Della wouldn't admit it. Too bad."

She gasped. "You killed Della?"

"Let's just say she's meeting with an accident soon. They can't get me for Laurie's murder, or your husband's, but they can get me for the drug operation, and I'm not going to prison."

"You killed Laurie Detry?" He had. She was certain.

He smirked. "She found out about my drug operation and threatened me unless I cut her in. Wrong, Laurie." He shook his head as if remembering, and grinned. "Nobody threatens me."

His ego. It was his passion—everybody had one. She catered

to it. "I believe you," she said, acting impressed and hating that she had to. "But why did you leave the gun behind? That's not like you."

"I heard Detry at the door, dropped it and hid. Idiot didn't even try to look for an intruder. He was all broken up over her, and called 911. Haggis found me, though. I told him to get rid of the Colt and distract you so I could get out.

"Only the idiot ultimately decided he couldn't take the guilt. No more letting you take the blame for the missing weapon. I came to his house to talk sense into him and heard him on the phone with you. I had just enough time to get rid of him before I heard the sirens."

He was a sick, mean individual. Angie didn't want to talk to him anymore, but she had to.

"Why did Cliff help you? I don't understand."

"He had debts, and his wife got cancer, and he had to pay some bills for her. So he went to work for my drug operation. He's not stupid. He did anything I told him to. Like taking care of your husband for me."

Angie's stomach turned over. That's why Cliff had been so kind to her? Because of the guilt he felt over killing Tony?

Gregg stopped at a red light, looked outside at the array of downtown Copper City shops and scowled. "The papers," he demanded again.

"Why on earth do you want them? There's nothing in that folder."

"Don't cross me, Angie. I'm warning you. Just tell me where the papers are!"

The light turned green, and Gregg took off.

"You're going to kill me the second you get the file, aren't you?"

"I don't leave any witnesses. You're the only one who can connect me to the murders, Angie."

"Then at least tell me why you sent Thatcher to shoot me before I even got the file."

"I thought Haggis had buried the papers I need with the gun, and that you'd dug them up. I never looked in his expense folder. When Santiago said you were snooping around the office, I checked and that folder was missing."

"Then why go after the woman at the cemetery?"

"I was after the surveillance disk, too, at first. Thatcher took her to make her tell where it was, but she wouldn't, so I told him to scare both of you by dropping her off in your car. Then I decided the disk didn't matter. The second time I thought you were hiding Haggis's papers with her. By then she knew too much. So do you."

"But those papers are only code and numbers."

"That can lead to my conviction, along with your testimony. I have someone I want to protect. Tell me where they are, or die in five minutes when we reach the station and you're picked off by a sniper while getting out of the vehicle along with Della. Your choice."

"They'll get you for kidnapping me."

He shook his head. "You made a false arrest, and then resisted arrest. I was taking you in. Now tell me where those papers are, or the sniper kills you in a random act of violence. Or two acts, counting Della. Home free."

Angie shivered. She'd blown everything. Just because of something she'd thought she'd seen in Detry's eyes, she'd stubbornly let her emotions rule her where an innocent man was concerned. Detry had loved his wife and he'd done nothing to Angie. Just raised his arm to her earlier, maybe out of frustration. Chloe had bruises because Detry had saved her life. Poor Ida had been right after all—Warren Detry was a different man than the one who had killed her daughter.

She'd cast a dark gloom over Chloe's wedding and lost Boone, all because she felt God was leading her to something that was only her imagination. She needed to start all over again with God.

And with Boone. He'd been right, too. She needed to live to tell him that, get her life back on track and ask his forgiveness. She hadn't forgiven him like she'd thought, because she'd been blind.

No more.

Gregg started through another intersection. A van cut in front of him and stopped, and he slammed on his brakes and swerved to avoid hitting it.

Swearing, he tried backing up, but he couldn't. They were blocked in by a police cruiser in back, and what looked like a SWAT team launching itself from the van in front.

"Walker set me up!" Gregg screamed at her. "Now you have to die." He reached for his gun.

Angie grabbed the door handle and pushed, flinging herself out of the car just as Gregg's gun boomed.

ELEVEN

The bullet whizzed above her as she hit the asphalt, her right arm groaning under her. More gunshots exploded around her. Glass broke, voices yelled. She closed her eyes tightly and prayed, too winded by the fall to try to get to safety.

Strong arms lifted her straight up off the ground, and she finally opened her eyes. Boone had her, was scanning her anxiously.

"He said you set him up," she said, scorn in her voice. "Do you believe the audacity?"

"She's cuffed!" Boone yelled to the bustling men around him. "Somebody get the key!" He turned back and pulled her against his chest, supporting a lot of her weight.

"I can stand," she protested. He hadn't answered her question, and she didn't understand why. He just held her.

"You're shaking," she added.

"That's you, Angel," Boone said, but she could hear gentle amusement in his voice. "Are you okay?"

"I will be as soon as someone gets the cuffs off."

"At your service," Jack said to the side of her. She watched him as he unlocked the restraints and took them away, holding them like a piece of evidence. They probably were.

She pulled away from Boone, testing her wobbly legs. They'd

hold. She flexed her shoulders, still dazed. Her arm hurt where she'd hit the ground, but that was probably just a bruise like the ones forming on her wrists and her other arm. Still, she was alive. She'd make it.

"Gregg?"

"He shouldn't have tried to kill you, Angie," Jack said. "We didn't have a choice."

She nodded solemnly, and then she remembered. "You've got to find Della, his secretary. Gregg said he set up a sniper at the Copper City PD to kill her and me both in the next five minutes."

She rested against Boone's chest as Jack called it in, taking deep breaths and thanking God she was alive.

Jack finally looked up. "They've got Della safe. The sniper's cornered. What else did Gregg say, Angie?"

The words poured out of her as she filled in the two men on everything, ending with, "He thought we dug up the papers in Cliff's file, and that's what he was trying to kill me to get. He wanted them to protect somebody?"

"Yeah, himself and his son." Boone nodded. "Drug enforcement thinks the code on Cliff's receipts pertains to who was selling what. Cliff might have kept track as evidence to get Gregg. They're trying to crack Santiago now."

This was horrible. She took a deep, shuddering breath. "Gregg also said you set him up?"

Boone and Jack exchanged a look, and Boone shook his head ever so slightly. She would have asked them what was going on, but it seemed like too much effort. Instead, she gave in, finally, and broke into sobs.

He held her close, stroking her hair, murmuring something to her. She didn't know what, didn't care. He was there, and that's all that mattered.

She finally got herself together and pulled away from Boone.

Jack was still there, gazing at Boone with a rare solemn look on his face.

"Did he say anything else?" the chief deputy asked.

"That I shouldn't have talked to Cliff or in court. Or to him about God."

To her surprise, Boone didn't smile. "He told you about Tony's death, and you still talked to him about God?"

She shook her head. "I did that before he told me. Good thing, too, because after, I wouldn't have. I think I just made him more angry anyway," she said, mopping at her eyes with her sleeves. "For certain, I didn't do any good."

"Maybe not with him." Boone handed her a tissue. "But you've got me praying."

Watching Jack turn away to phone someone, Angie wiped her cheeks and tried not to look surprised. She knew God was powerful. He'd turned her whole life around. Still, Boone seemed a harder case than she'd been.

"Praying for what?" she asked him.

"For you not to be hurt." Boone took her in his arms again.

"Do you think it helped?" she asked, reaching around his waist to hug him. She lay her cheek on the soft cotton of his button-down shirt.

"You're here. I guess that tells me something."

If Boone's effort to trust in God was the only reason she'd had to suffer through all this with Gregg, well, she'd gladly do it again. She now had hope. Separating from him, she gazed into his eyes and took his hand, sensing the bond they had growing stronger.

That was why God thought it so important not to be unequally yoked, she realized. This feeling of Boone understanding her beliefs, even if just a little bit, was priceless.

Jack shut off his phone and turned back to them, just as Boone warned her, "It might not mean anything, my praying."

"It's a start."

"You two are getting too intense for me." Jack said. "Boone—your bodyguard has been released, charges dropped."

Angie narrowed her eyes, trying to put two and two together. "What bodyguard, and how come it wasn't you doing the guarding?"

"I'll explain later," Boone told her.

"Yeah, you will."

Jack waved to get her attention because she was still eyeing Boone with suspicion. She turned to Jack and raised an eyebrow.

"The sniper's been caught. Since you're obviously feeling good enough to fight with us, I'll assume you're up to telling us how Gregg got your weapon and badge?"

"Absolutely," she said. She let go of Boone and turned to Jack. "But I need to warn you, you aren't going to be happy."

"How do you put up with this?" Jack asked Boone.

"I like being warned ahead of time I'm going to be mad," Boone teased, but concern remained in his eyes. "Besides, it's part of her charm."

Before they could continue their two-man show, Angie told them about Detry and how the chief had come upon them. "Gregg nullified the arrest, and let Detry go. He told me I was suspended, and that I had to hand over my duty weapon and my badge. I walked away. He caught up to me by the car and cuffed me, and the rest you know."

"I hope you don't want to pursue the arrest." Jack's frown told Angie she'd been right. He wasn't at all happy.

"No."

"Good." Jack finished writing and shut his notebook.

"But I would like my duty weapon and badge back," she said. "Unless his suspension is binding."

"I don't think there will be a problem. I'll talk to whoever gets named acting chief and let you know," Jack said, closing his notebook. "I have everything I'll need for right now. The car should be okay to drive to a shop. Nothing crunched but the bumper."

"Ida is going to be so pleased," Angie said, watching until Jack was out of earshot. She gave herself a shake, her eyes on Boone. "Spill it. Why did you put a bodyguard on me this morning?"

Around them, the sheriff's department worked gathering evidence, directing traffic and fending off news reporters. Boone moved her to the sidewalk next to a tea shop and away from bystanders as the officers began to clear the road to help the flow of traffic.

He chose his words carefully. "After the way we left each other, I don't really have to tell you anything."

She grinned at him. "Yeah, but you know you want to."

His mouth edged into a small, worried grin of his own. "I hired the bodyguard because the sheriff's department was arresting Gregg this morning, and I was worried he would come after you. I was right."

"I thought someone was following me from Ida's," she said, thinking back to before the funeral, "but I gave him the slip."

"That was the bodyguard."

"But I never saw Gregg until I was arresting Detry." Her nerves crackled at the thought that Gregg was following her. "Is the man you hired all right?"

"Yes. Gregg arrested him on a trumped-up charge, got him out of there and came after you at the funeral. I don't know how he figured out who my guy was."

It didn't matter anyway. It was over. "I was wrong about Detry," she said softly. "I don't have to be afraid for Chloe anymore."

To say Boone looked thrilled wouldn't do his expression justice. "Excellent. Now you can go talk to your mother and clear up whatever the problem is between you two, and then…" He stopped speaking.

He had such hope in his eyes. She wanted to say yes, but she was still afraid.

"Mr. Walker, I hate to bust in, but do you need a ride home?"

Angie turned. It was Sonny. She flashed on the van she'd seen cut in front of Gregg at the intersection and the word *glass* on the side of it. Sonny's van. She realized he must have been helping out the sheriff's department. Which was really strange, because they had their own vans.

"What a coincidence," she said. "Or did Jack already call you to tow Ida's car?"

"I was waiting for—"

"That's okay, Sonny," Boone broke in. "We're driving Ida's car back to my garage so Angie and I can get our vehicles. I'd appreciate it if you would tow it from there."

Sonny nodded. "I'll take care of it." He turned to leave.

Angie put her hand on Sonny's thick arm, stopping him. "Who were you waiting for, and I know you don't need Boone's permission to speak."

"I was waiting to see if Mr. Walker needed a ride." He pointed to his van, parked in front of the deli.

He wasn't there to tow them, then. "Why would you think Boone would need a ride?"

Sonny hesitated.

He was protecting Boone, she realized. Okay. That made sense. She tilted her head up to look at the man she was just about in love with. Most of the time.

"What are you hiding?"

"He drove Jack and me here."

So he'd arrived with the SWAT team. She waved her hand at him in a "please continue" gesture.

"Sonny backed Jack and me up earlier when we attempted to capture Gregg at the cemetery. We set him up, offering to exchange the disk for his calling the dogs off you and leaving town. He didn't fall for it and came after you instead."

She tried to put this together in her head. And when she added foreknowledge and plan together, she came up with one word. Control.

Boone had done it again.

"You couldn't warn me ahead of time the man was dangerous?" She felt her face warm as she flashed her eyes at him.

"I told you to stay at Ida's and not to go to the funeral," Boone argued. "I figured we'd arrest Gregg, and you'd be safe."

She threw her hands in the air. "I let him take my gun, Boone, because I didn't have a clue."

"She sounds mad. I'm outta here." Sonny waved his hand and fled.

Boone ignored his friend, his gaze focused on her. "I was worried you'd go after him yourself if you knew."

"That's why you hired the bodyguard. To make sure I didn't."

"Everything worked out fine," he evaded. "Your pastor called in the kidnapping, and we found you in time."

"Gregg came within seconds of killing me! Just like with everything else in your life, you had to do what *you* thought was best. Your way. You didn't trust me. You won't trust anyone but yourself."

Boone might as well have pulled a shade down over his face, so completely did he mask what he was thinking. She hated that.

"If I had come to you first, would you have gone after Gregg yourself?" he asked.

"I don't know," she admitted. "But that isn't the point."

"Sure it is. I was protecting you the best I knew how, and that's what you asked me to do. If you had found out he was the one who sent the men after you, you might well have gone after him alone, and the outcome might have been worse. Especially if you'd had a gun when he admitted to murdering Tony."

"You don't see it, do you? I could have been prepared if you'd warned me, and not ended up on the asphalt with a bullet going off over my head. You rescued me in time, but that was *God* working, not you."

His mouth worked back and forth. "Okay. I'm sorry. I made a mistake. But I had to try to protect you."

She didn't know what to say. She couldn't tell him it was okay, because he would keep doing it over and over again.

"We all make mistakes," Boone pointed out. "You wanted to hang Detry, and I still love you."

"There's a big difference," she said. "I talked to you about what I was going to do in Newton. You didn't talk this over with me. Because of your need to be in control.

"But you can't be in control of my life or even your own, and direct everything into a good outcome. Only God can. If you can't see that and begin to trust Him instead of yourself, you're not ever going to change."

"I don't know that I'll ever be able to give control of my life over to something I can only barely comprehend or trust."

He was resolute. Gone was any hope she'd had of making their relationship work, now that she was willing to stop going after Detry and face her life. She bit down on her lip. She loved him. She wanted to put her arms around him, lean on him, let him be her rock and direct her whole life. But she couldn't. It wouldn't work.

"I think we'd best go our separate ways, Boone. We'll only make each other unhappy if we stay together."

"That's what you want?"

"It's what's best."

He looked hurt, which made her want to cry. But she had to remain strong. "You still want me to drive you back to your office?"

"Just answer one question for me, and then I'll tell you. If you forgave me, you'd have to put yourself out to be loved. You sure you're not just using this as an excuse to run away from love again? Too afraid it will fail you again if you try?"

"Of course I'm not."

"Did you talk to your mother yet?"

Her mouth went tight. "That's two questions."

"That's what I thought."

Was she running from Boone's love, or running toward God's promises? Was this a matter of just not forgiving people? She shook her head, confused. She had to call it quits with Boone, or with God. She couldn't take this turmoil much longer.

"I'll ride with Jack," he told her, turning.

"Fine," she said, but she wasn't sure he heard her. He was walking away too quickly.

Striding toward Sonny, who was waiting in his van until the police car in his way cleared out, Angie asked him to send a tow for Ida's car now and take her to his shop. He could send someone after her own wheels. She didn't want to chance running into Boone again, but she didn't tell Sonny that.

She didn't have to. He was sure he could tell by the tears in her eyes.

Angie didn't end up crying. She refused to. This was not her fault. Instead, she got busy trying to repair what was left of her life. She left a message on Ida's machine, saying she had found out she was wrong about Detry after all, and that with Gregg no longer a threat, she was going back to her apartment. She'd be in touch after she mended fences with her family.

The next day, the acting chief called and she sat through a morning of questions and answers. She received her gun and badge back, with the acting chief's apologies. He also told her she'd acted commendably, and he was proud to have her in the department. She wanted to call Boone and tell him. She didn't.

When she got home, she stayed busy cleaning and unpacking her suitcase and the garment bag she'd brought home with her from Ida's before the funeral. Then she had nothing left to do but sit on her bed and try to figure out what to wear to the wedding rehearsal. And think.

The truth was, she was not looking forward to apologizing to Detry and Chloe and was putting off getting to Newton early. What if they told her it was too late? Could she bear being left with no one who really loved her?

God did, she reminded herself. It would have to be enough. Boone was right. She was trying to escape being hurt again, and she couldn't. Her own stubbornness and inability to forgive had brought loneliness on her for many years, and she had to overcome both.

Still undecided on what to wear, she finished with her curling iron as the phone chirped. Sonny. Ida's car would be ready at noon the next day. She told him she'd let Ida know, and that she, Angie, would pay any amount the insurance didn't. He told her not to worry—Boone had already covered the whole thing, since, Boone said, it was his fault.

She hung up, and sank down onto her bed, sadness flooding over her again. Boone was a man in a million. He meant well. But if she stayed, they would be at odds forever, and neither of them would be happy. She couldn't do that to him.

She couldn't think about Boone now.

"Whatever is lovely, whatever is true, whatever is pure…dwell on these things." Not the right order of the verse, but close—and it worked. She felt calmer. She ought to memorize more Scripture. She felt the need to get closer to God.

The phone chirped at five-thirty. She was late, but it was Ida calling from the biker bar, so she answered. Just the sound of her "hello" made Angie feel a little better. Maybe she wasn't totally alone, not with a friend like Ida.

"I'm glad you called," she told Ida, smiling. "Your car is ready, and it's paid for."

"Lemme guess. The eye magnet."

Her heart clenched at the mere mention of Boone's nickname. She still had it bad.

"Yeah," she said, her throat dry.

"Now my news. Hold on." Ida shouted something to someone about holding down the fort for her, and then a dozen seconds later, the background noise lessened.

"Listen, baby, I knew I was right about Detry. But after everything that happened, before I tried to convince you again, I knew I would need proof. So Rick and I drove to Butterfield, where you told me Detry claimed he grew up in that court document? In the cemetery there, we found the name Warren Detry. The gravestone said the man was only nine months younger than Donaldson. He died in some football accident while he was away in college. Get this. He was Donaldson's cousin. They were born the same year and looked a lot alike. If someone asked about Detry, he'd get the poor kid's history, not Wayne Donaldson's, who never even lived there. And someone might not think to mention he died."

Angie listened, stunned, while Ida took a breath. Before she could figure out what to say, Ida continued.

"Whew! That's more than I ever said at one time. I made double sure it wasn't a messed-up identification. The real Detry was identified through his teeth and a tattoo he got in college, which Donaldson couldn't have known about. The real Detry is really dead. Under no circumstances can you let your sister marry Wayne Donaldson. He's dangerous. Explosive. I know it, and somewhere inside, you know it, too."

Angie blinked, the picture of Detry raising his hand to strike her at the funeral coming to her unbidden. And something else. The fury in his eyes she kept seeing—had seen since she'd first laid eyes on him.

"Ida, is there something you're not telling me?" she whispered.

"Yep, there is. Have you talked to your mother yet?"

"Yes. We've said 'Hello,' 'goodbye' and 'how are you,' basically."

"Talk to your mother. Then you'll understand." Ida dragged in a breath.

"Just tell me, Ida."

"I can't. I made a promise. Go, talk to your mother, tell her about me, about Detry and Donaldson, and save your sister. And bring the hero with you for protection."

"No can do, Ida, on the last. But I'll be working on the others." She disconnected.

Angie set the phone down. Looking up, she saw her own face, and the bruises on her arm from the previous morning. They reminded her of her sister's bruises.

Detry *had* put them there. She knew that now, just as surely as she knew that talking to her mother might be the clue in ironing out everything between them—and saving her sister's life.

God had made everything come together. He was giving her another chance at getting back her family, now that she'd lost Boone.

Leaping up, she dressed for danger as fast as she could, grabbed her purse and headed toward her bright orange car.

Boone was poring over the paperwork he'd badly neglected during the last few days, but the image of Angie and her sad green eyes kept leaping back into his mind. He shoved aside the papers in disgust.

He loved her. He adored her, for that matter. But he couldn't change for her. He had to keep control of things. If his father had, he would never have gone to prison and left his mother and him to fend for themselves. His mother had counted on God for a while, but then God had let her down. That was why he couldn't depend on God. He didn't trust God to make him or anyone he loved happy.

The phone's ringing jagged through his brain. It was after five, so Karen was gone. He picked it up and barked, "What?" into the mouthpiece.

"I must have the wrong number. I'm looking for the eye magnet, and he doesn't talk like that."

"Sorry, Ida." He'd recognize her voice anywhere. "I'm just not in a good mood right now. What can I do for you?"

"Angie needs your help right now. She refused to call you. I got pretty convincing proof that the man who murdered my daughter changed his name to Warren Detry, and she's taking him down."

Alarm coursed through his body. This did not sound good. "Taking him down how, exactly?"

"I told her to go talk to her mother about her past. Her mother is the key to this all, Boone. But I can't tell her what I know until her mother talks to her. I made a promise a long time ago."

"You didn't make a promise to me, Ida. Spill it."

There was a long silence, then Ida did. Boone put down his pen and listened, growing increasingly worried.

"So you see, after Angie and her mother talk, and Angie explains about me and what I found out about Detry's real identity, I know her mother is going to help her break up the wedding, and Detry is going to get furious, just like he did when my daughter—"

"I get it." Boone unlocked his desk drawer where he kept his weapon and pulled it out. "I'm going."

"You gonna save her and then marry her, right?" Ida asked hopefully.

He gave an edgy laugh as he slipped his Glock into his holster. "I thought we were a divorce waiting to happen," he said. "That's what you told Angie, right?"

"That was before I got to know you. Now I think you're perfect for each other."

"Don't ever try to make money matchmaking, Ida," he advised glumly. "As for saving her, I'm on my way."

He broke the connection and headed for the door. He didn't know what Angie would say about his interference, but he couldn't just sit here if she needed help.

He loved her. He really loved her, more than his career. More than anything.

He'd been wrong about Detry. Sure, he hadn't killed his wife, but he was dangerous, and Angie had known it, deep down in her heart, and he should have listened to her. And if she was right about Detry, was she right about God?

Suddenly, he had to know.

He started praying as he slammed out of his office and ran to the garage.

TWELVE

Edgy, her eyes watching out for Detry, Angie stepped into the church she'd attended as a child. Immediately she heard laughter coming from the fellowship hall, where she presumed the rehearsal dinner was going on. He'd be there, then. Instead of going left to join the gathering, she made a right and walked into the sanctuary.

Sinking onto the front pew, Angie kept her bag clutched to her. The huge old clock on the wall *tick, tick, ticked* away the seconds till the wedding, making her more nervous. She'd debated the whole hour-long drive there, but in the end, she knew she couldn't interrupt the rehearsal or the dinner, no matter how urgent this was. If Chloe got upset at her presence, Madeleine might get angry, and she would lose the chance to talk to her mother and find out whatever this key was that Madeleine held to everything. She couldn't risk it.

She could smell the enticing aromas of the meal and hear people laughing through the hallway. Her stomach growled. She wanted to go in, be a part of that, be one of the family. But she couldn't. She had to save someone who wouldn't save herself from what could be a terrible future. Deep inside, she knew Detry was a time bomb waiting to explode, and she couldn't risk being around him and triggering him.

Lord, I put my faith in You, she prayed silently. *Somehow, please, make this all come out right. Help me to do what is best.* Other desires replayed in her heart. A future with Boone and a family of their own. Both seemed impossible to achieve, nowhere within reach, so she didn't pray for them. She was afraid if God didn't answer her prayers that she would run from Him like she'd run from everything else that hurt her.

Ten minutes passed and finally, the ever-present buzz of voices from the fellowship hall got louder, then faded. She rose and walked to the door to peek out. People trickled toward the exit. The dinner was over.

It was time.

She watched for her mother to leave as the last of the bridesmaids exited the building minutes later, but no one else came out. Praying she didn't run into Detry, who had yet to leave, she went through the familiar hallway to the large hall at the rear of the building and stopped at the door. Chloe and Detry stood speaking with the pastor at the far end of the hall, and Angie rushed to get out of their sight in the kitchen, where she heard other voices.

Madeleine was chatting with three other women as they loaded the dishwasher and didn't notice her at the door until one of the other ladies smiled.

"Angie! Your mother told us you had some police duties to do and might not make it. We're so glad to see you. Fix yourself a dish."

"Thank you, Mrs. Marquez. I can't right now. Mom, can we talk for a few seconds in private?"

Madeleine nodded and joined her, and they headed into the hallway. Angie didn't look to see if Chloe or Detry noticed them. She closed the door. Her heart thumped so fast she could hear blood whooshing in her ears. If Madeleine said no, it was all over.

"This is life or death. I have to talk to you without Chloe or Detry around."

"What for?" Madeleine's brown eyes surveyed her with almost a critical slant to them. Angie sensed she wanted to say no.

"Ida Zlotsky sent me. She said you need to tell me about the past."

Her mother backed up against the paneled wall. Her hand went to her heart, and she swayed. Chloe reached out to her, and her mother grabbed her arm for support.

"Mom?"

"I'm all right. Go to my house. I'll be following you as soon as I grab my purse. Chloe and Warren are heading to another engagement party after they leave here, so we should be alone."

"Are you all right to drive?"

Madeleine drew in a deep breath and nodded slowly. Standing up straight, she pushed back her shoulders. "Go ahead. I'll follow. I would ride with you and explain everything, but this is better done at the house."

The short drive back to her childhood home seemed endless. Her mother knew Ida. How? Why? Something to do with her. But what? It couldn't be good, not if it was something to bury for all these years.

Buried past, buried evidence, buried love. So much of her life had all been buried under a thick layer of hurt. It was time to dig again. What was going to be unearthed, she didn't know, but she knew she was scared.

She parked the car in the driveway under the overhead lamp and briefly considered waiting on the porch, which had chairs. Her mother had left the front light on, though, and she would feel like a target. Instead, she went around to the rear entrance. No seats out here, but in the dark she'd be hidden.

Her mother's car pulling in made her step back into the light of the driveway so she wouldn't frighten her again. But Madeleine seemed to have pulled herself together. She gave Angie a grim smile as she locked the car and strode up to the door, letting them both into the living room.

"I left the back door unlocked; you could have gotten in that way," Madeleine said.

"You shouldn't do that, Mom."

"I know." She pulled her elegantly manicured nails through her silver-streaked blond hair. "Sit on the couch. I'll get the bag."

Angie didn't ask what bag. A minute later, her mother joined her on the couch and sat down with a faded pink, quilted baby bag frayed at the ends.

"This was yours." She unzipped it and pulled out a hand-made rag doll dressed in a red, white and blue shirt, blue pants and red booties that looked like sneakers. Angie blinked at a sudden memory.

Instinctively, she reached for it, turning it over and over in her hands. "I don't remember the doll, but I remember seeing a picture of me as a little girl in a Fourth of July set just like this. What was I—three years old?"

Her mother nodded, looking down at the bag. "You loved to dress your dolls in clothes they could play outside in." She handed Angie a pink doll dress and booties from the bag. "These were in the bag when you first came. They were stained already, and I always meant to wash them, but when you wouldn't play with the doll, I put it away in the bag and forgot."

"What do you mean, when I first came?"

Madeleine finally met her gaze. She pressed her lips together. "I kept the doll and clothes because they were handmade," she said, not answering her question. "Someone must have loved you tremendously to do that."

Pain cascaded in her chest. Someone, but not Madeleine.

"You were dressed just like this doll is now when you were brought here."

"I was adopted?" she asked, her heart ceasing to beat for a few seconds. She didn't understand. If she was wanted like that— why had her mother been so remote? "You and Dad weren't my real parents?"

"Your dad was." The older woman bit down on her lip, turned to get a tissue out of the box on the coffee table, and dabbed at her eyes. "He had an affair with an eighteen-year-old he met out on the road, driving those…trucks." She said *trucks* as if it was a bad word. "We had a knock on the door in the middle of the night, and we opened it to find you, with this bag and a note."

Angie put the doll aside on the couch. She was trying to understand, but it was hard. "What did the note say?"

"It was from your grandmother. It said you were in danger. That your mom was murdered, and she couldn't keep you, even though she wanted to. To hide you and start using your father's last name. It was signed—"

"Ida," Angie said along with her. Ida was her grandmother? Despite Chloe's life being in danger, despite her mother's tears, Angie smiled. But only for a second.

"Your dad moved us out of town immediately, all the way down to Kentucky for a long while. We had financial problems from having to move so suddenly. I was angry over that, and because I had to give up being practically next door to my mom and dad, my sisters and my church, which I loved. My whole life was different, and it was hard to start again. Your dad went on the road more because I was so angry at him. Plus every time I looked at you, I remembered he had an affair, because you didn't look like him. You must have taken after your birth mother."

That was why Detry had given her such a strange look when he'd first seen her. And by the church, when he'd been surprised she didn't know something—this was it. He was surprised she didn't remember he killed her mother.

Angie's head spun.

Tears rolled down Madeleine's cheeks again. "I'm sorry I was like I was, Angie. You're were only three when you came to us, and I have no excuse. I should have gotten over it, but I never did forgive him, a fact that I have regretted every second since he died. Carrying that grudge made me hard, and you suffered."

Angie leaned over the baby bag and hugged her. "It's okay. I forgive you." She truly did. But when she pulled away and looked at the face of the woman who'd raised her, she saw Madeleine's dark brown eyes held doubt. "It really is okay. We all make mistakes." Boone had said that.

Boone. He was going to hate finding out she'd been right about Detry after all.

"Thank you." Her mother's face softened. "I have your blanket you brought with you in here, too," she said, patting the baby bag. "But you said something about life or death?"

Chloe. She worked her bottom lip. "I've got to tell you this. Please try to believe me. Ida has been searching for the man who murdered her daughter." She paused. "My birth mother."

Madeleine waved her hand in the air. "Go on."

"My mother was murdered in her little rental house. Ida suspects my mother's boyfriend did it, then started a couple of major fires to cover it up. The fire spread and took out the block, including a factory that employed a lot of the town and a biker bar. Old buildings, they went up fast." Ida had told her that.

"How did you get free?" Madeleine asked with a gasp.

"I don't remember." If she hadn't been at Ida's, she suspected she might have wandered to Ida's house, or maybe Ida came and found her and her mother as the fire got going and rescued her.

"Donaldson—the boyfriend—disappeared that night. Today, Ida found out he had a cousin the same age, with similar features, named Warren Detry."

Madeleine frowned.

"The real Warren Detry died when he was twenty-one. Chloe's fiancé is Wayne Donaldson, the man who murdered my mother."

Madeline's eyes were horrified. "Are you certain?"

"Ida is. And it's the only thing that makes sense. Donaldson told Boone he was Warren Detry from Butterfield, where a background check would have brought up Detry's good history. But Donaldson slipped up and told Chloe he was from Colleyville, where my mother died. Boone and I went there. No one knew the Warren Detry name. Plus Ida says the deceased Warren Detry was identified positively by his teeth and a tattoo on his arm."

"Warren—Donaldson—told Chloe he hates tattoos," Madeleine said. "My poor baby." Her face crumpled. Slowly, she shook her head, then suddenly, she gasped.

"Oh, my. I might have other proof." Reaching into the pink bag again, she pulled out a worn pink comforter, with a baby face imprint on one corner. On a different one were dark stains.

Angie went cold inside. She could barely breathe, and she didn't understand why.

"I always thought those were paint," Madeleine said. "But if it was from the night your mother was murdered, it might be…" Her voice trailed off.

"Blood," Angie said, horrified. She sat up straight. "We have to get this to the police. If Donaldson's DNA is on it, it would be the proof we need—"

"That was supposed to have burned in the fire," a deep voice interrupted from behind Angie.

Detry. In one smooth movement, Angie whipped her gun from its holster, rose and turned around in front of Madeleine, to shield her.

He'd murdered her mother. She wasn't giving him a chance to murder anyone else.

"Madeleine, leave. Quickly," she said without turning her head. *Lord, please make her obey*. Her gaze pinned to Detry, she commanded, "Put down your weapon."

Angie sensed Madeleine moving behind her. Heard her heels tap on the wooden floor.

"Stay," Donaldson shouted. Madeleine uttered a startled cry. *Focus,* Angie told herself. His gun wavered in the air.

"Put down your weapon," she repeated.

He gazed back and forth between her and her mother, misery and anger mixed on his face. She might be able to appeal to his misery. Make him think everything could get better her way, not his. If she could, fine, but she was fully prepared to go for his weapon if it bought Madeleine time to get away. That was, unless he'd hurt Chloe. If he had, she might shoot him now.

"Where's Chloe?"

"She's at the party. I told her I had to get something and not to leave till I returned."

Relief flooded her. "Good. Then let's not make everything worse. Put down the gun, Wayne." She used his real name to see if she could bring him to reality.

Big mistake.

His face reddening, he shook his head adamantly. "Don't call me that. I'm not him anymore. I haven't been for a long time. I fixed my life."

"Okay. Warren." She kept her gun steady. His weapon alternated between steady and waving at her. At Madeleine. Neither was good. She had to calm him down, not make him angry. He struck when angry.

"You've only done one crime. You were young. You're obviously sorry. So put the gun down." Keep him talking, she told herself. Wear out his anger. Pretend it wasn't your mother he hurt. She swallowed down a tightening throat. "I don't want anything to happen to any of us."

"You don't care about me," he retorted.

"Of course I care. You're the only one who can tell me what my mother did to make you so angry. I need to know."

She needed to, but she didn't want to. She was afraid to know. She was just buying time, praying that Madeleine would get a chance to escape. She edged sideways so she'd be free of the couch, in front of Madeleine.

"Stop moving!"

"Tell me what happened," she said, stopping where she was. He didn't think to order her back to her original position.

Without speaking, he gazed past her to the windows. He couldn't see out. They were both covered with opaque drapes. They always had been—she didn't have to look. His breathing rapid, his face sweaty, she figured he could crack at any minute. She might have to shoot him.

Could she ever mentally prepare herself for that?

"Your mother led me to believe you were my daughter," he said without looking into her eyes.

Her heart slammed to a stop. She reminded herself that she wasn't his blood, and the beat returned to normal.

"I believed you were for three years," he continued. "I loved you as my daughter. Then she told me you weren't."

"How old were you?"

"I was seventeen when we met. She was nineteen. She'd already gotten pregnant by your real father." He glanced at Madeleine, so he must have realized the connection. "She didn't want to get him in trouble. So she picked me out to use."

"Use how?" Angie asked.

"I was a dropout, father dead, kicked out of my mother's house, but I was smart enough to get a room and make good money doing construction work. She needed the money. I wanted the family. We were happy for three years. Then she decided she wanted to get rid of me and told me the truth. That you weren't my daughter. I got mad. Hit her. She fought back. Then I couldn't stop hitting her." His words were coming faster now. "You saw the whole thing."

His eyes. That had to be when she'd seen the fury in his eyes for the very first time. Each time she'd thought she'd seen murder in his eyes, she had, but it was the memory from the murder of her mother, not of Laurie Detry.

"You ran out. I thought I'd hide everything with a big fire. They would think the fire killed her. Went to find you, to bring you with me. We could be a family."

She sucked in a breath at the thought.

"Your grandmother took you, I think. I couldn't find you."

Ida had brought her to safety to save her life. If she'd remained with Ida, Detry would have always known how to get to her. Emotion overwhelmed her. She shook her head, hard, to stave off tears that would cloud her eyes and her reaction time. Okay, she was a crier.

"It was a crime of passion," she said slowly, not wanting to give him hope at all. But she had to. She had to protect Madeleine. "You were young. You've changed. You might even plead down to a manslaughter charge."

"Can't risk it." Detry's swiped away sweat from his brow, his gaze not leaving her. "Can't risk losing Chloe. I'm going to have to kill you. I don't want to, but I don't have a choice. If I let you go, Chloe might not believe you, but she'll listen to Madeleine. Plus you have the blanket."

His blood must be on it, or he wouldn't be worried.

"I was surprised you didn't remember that night," Detry added. His voice had lost emotion. Not a good sign.

Don't give up, Angie thought. Keep him talking.

"Are you going to hurt Chloe, too?" she asked.

"She's my family. I'm taking her off from the party to elope." His arm stiffened as he raised his gun.

"You'll hurt her when she finds out you killed us." Angie started moving sideways again.

"She'll think it was the men who were after you." He stiffened his arms to shoot.

"Wait!" Angie demanded. "What about God? You became a Christian. God wouldn't want you to do this."

His arms slackened. He blinked rapidly, considering what she'd said.

"God won't forgive my murdering Belinda."

Angie drew a sharp breath. Her mother's name had been Belinda. "Yes, He will," she forced herself to say. "You're God's child. You're sorry it happened. Your past sins are forgiven."

"Chloe said you're a Christian. Do you forgive me?"

She blinked. For murdering her mother? For making her lose the life she could have had with her real mother and Ida as a grandmother? For putting her in a position where she had to doubt her ability to be a mother?

For almost ruining her life?

She'd been able to forgive Madeleine easily, because she understood why the woman had acted toward her as she had. But Chief Gregg and Detry—they'd done irreparable harm to her in one way or another.

Did she really have to forgive them?

She didn't know about Gregg, but Detry still professed to be a Christian. He was sorry, and he'd just asked her for forgiveness. God said she had to forgive, seventy times seven. She didn't want to. But she knew better than to rebel.

"I forgive you," she said. "Now show God you really are sorry, and put down your gun."

He shook his head. "Put down your gun, prove you're serious about forgiving me first."

That was the last thing she'd expected. Every instinct told her not to do it. Her weapon was the only thing stopping him from murdering them both.

Or maybe it was the only thing standing in the way of Wayne Donaldson finally seeing God's love through her forgiveness. Moving in slow motion, she put the weapon on the end table at the side of the couch, and inched over to where she was freely facing him.

"I do forgive you, Wayne," she said. "Now put down *your* gun. Trust God to do what's best for you."

He wavered. "I'm sorry, but you're a witness—"

"Put down the weapon, Donaldson!" Angie said more forcefully.

The front door pushed open suddenly, diverting Donaldson's attention past her. Angie glanced behind her. Saw Ida at the door, gun in hand, ready.

"Drop it!" Ida shouted.

Anger exploded on Warren's face as he recognized the older woman. Angie knew. Knew he was going to shoot her grandmother. Her Grandma Ida.

She could not let that happen. She threw herself forward, toward him.

He shot. The bullet hit her full impact. Angie felt herself crumple. Heard Madeleine scream. Heard another shot crack the air in half. Her last prayer was for God to send Boone. She'd blown it. He was the only hope to save Ida and Madeleine now.

Boone swung open his car door at Madeleine's and was alerted by the fury of two gunshots inside the house. Fear of losing Angie tearing through him, he freed his weapon and hit the cement driveway running, up the walk, to the front door, each step taking a lifetime.

Leave everything to God. That's what Angie had said he should do. He spent the ride trying to understand how God could take care of everything for the good, and give him peace—but at this second, all he knew was fear. Soul-killing fear.

She's a good cop, he told himself. *Trust her.*

He did. Whom he didn't entirely trust was God.

He stood to one side of the open front door, his weapon ready. Through the screen, he could hear female voices in the living room. Madeleine and Ida. With Detry groaning.

But no Angie.

"Madeleine? You all right?" he called.

"It's Boone!" Ida said.

"Ida?" Boone called. "Where's Angie?"

"Come in, Boone." That was Madeleine. "Call the police for us. He shot her. Detry shot her."

Boone flung open the screen door.

Lord God, don't let her be dead. Please, don't let her be dead.

He rushed inside. Ida held a gun on Detry, who was seated on the floor just inside the kitchen, holding his shoulder. Angie lay on the floor with Madeleine kneeling beside her, cradling Angie's upper torso.

"Angel?" He strode to Madeleine's side, pulling out his phone and dialing for help. The second he saw Angie blinking, his heart started beating again.

She was alive. No blood. This was good.

"She'll be okay." Madeleine looked up, teary-eyed. "She said she's wearing her bulletproof vest. She saved Ida."

"Just winded," Angie whispered, then closed her eyes again. "But we're safe. You're here."

Boone started breathing again. He spoke to a woman on the phone who promised to get the police and an ambulance there immediately.

"Help's on its way," Boone told them. "Ida? You okay?"

"Sure," she said, but her voice was weak.

"Where's his gun?"

"It's under the table." She pointed to a spot about five feet away. Detry wasn't chancing Ida's wrath again. Boone was done worrying about anything but Angie, though. He hit his knees beside her and took her hand.

"Thank you, God," he said simply.

"I heard that," Angie said slowly, her eyebrows raising. "So I must still be unconscious, right?"

"If you are, I'm your dream date."

They shared a grin.

"Well, if you're back to making goo-goo eyes at Boone," Ida said, "I guess I don't have to worry about you."

"I never make goo-goo eyes at anyone," Angie protested, but the tips of her lips were still turned upward. "Ida, you called him by name."

Ida glanced at them, looking flustered. "A lapse. That's all it was. You got me flustered."

Madeleine looked from Angie to Boone. "You can watch over her?"

Boone nodded, holding back the word *forever* until he was certain Angie wanted to hear it.

"I'm going outside to call Chloe," Madeleine told them. That was something Boone was happy he didn't have to do. She let Boone lift Angie up into his arms and bring her to the couch, where he cradled her against him, then she retrieved her cell phone and left to go on the porch, leaving the main door open.

Boone turned his attention back to Angie.

"You came," she said softly, blinking those beautiful green eyes of hers, so full of life. "I knew you would."

"I didn't come in time."

"God didn't want you to."

"You got shot. You could have died. It was my fault. I should have listened to you about Detry."

"Well, if I'd known it was that easy to convince you, I would have let the guys in the Mustang shoot me. Then we wouldn't have had to go through all this." She chuckled, and then groaned. The pain wasn't her injury as much as the residual shock of getting shot, she figured. "I'm just kidding, you know."

"Yeah," Boone said, a bundle of emotions welling up in him. "I know."

The sirens sounded through the screen door, and she opened her eyes. "You're not leaving, are you?"

"You're kidding again, right?"

She smiled. "Right."

True to his word, after speaking to the police and Ida and finding out a bit more about what had happened before he had arrived, Boone rode in the ambulance with her to Newton Memorial, and only left her side when the nurses shooed him out so the doctors could check her over. She was bruised and sore, but she got out of there in what she considered record time, her spirits lifted when she found out Madeleine wanted her back home.

Her sister hugged her gently when she arrived, but then, subdued, went upstairs to her own room for the rest of the evening.

"I told her everything," Madeleine said in a hushed voice. She added, "Warren—um, Wayne—has been charged with attempted murder. That's just for starters. He confessed to your mother's beating right there, after they took you outside, and said he wanted to come clean, because you forgave him. And to tell you he knows it won't help, but he really is sorry."

Angie closed her eyes for a few seconds. Somehow, this evening, God had reached him. That was good.

Madeleine led them into the living room, where Ida, having remained to answer the questions the police had for her, rushed to Angie.

"Now that you're looking a little stronger, I can say this—I can't believe you took a bullet for me." Ida wrapped her arms around her, being careful not to hug her tightly. "What, you think seeing my granddaughter dead would be easier than getting shot? Are you crazy?"

"I love you, Ida," Angie said, smiling widely.

The older woman blushed. "I love you, too."

"I know."

Angie settled in the corner of the couch, propped up by pillows. Boone sat next to her, with Ida across from her. Madeleine and Ida had already cleaned up the scene, and Madeleine got iced tea for Boone and coffee for Angie.

Black and strong. She deserved that.

"You saved us, Ida," Angie said. "How did you know to come?"

"After I called you, I got this feeling." Ida pursed her mouth. She resembled a woman trying very hard not to cry as she gazed at Angie. "My posse couldn't make it, so I was only going to pass by and reassure myself everything was okay. But Boone wasn't here, and Donaldson's car was up the street." She gave an angry shake of her head. "I knew something was wrong, because why wouldn't he park in the driveway? So I snuck up here to the door and listened. When you yelled to put down the gun, I stopped listening." She took a deep breath. "The second you went down, I shot him before he could get Madeleine."

Ida's eyes went to Boone. "You'll be my lawyer, right?"

"Of course. But did the police say you'll need one?"

She shook her head. "They could change their minds and claim I had a vendetta. Of course, then I would have aimed for his heart. I just wanted him caught."

"You saved Madeleine's life, Ida," Angie reminded her. "And you saved mine twice. Once now, and once when I was little."

"I tried to save Belinda, too, that night," Ida told her, the pain of that memory on her face. "You walked the two blocks to my house, and told me your mommy was hurt. I left you with a neighbor and rushed over there, but the house was burning. I went inside to find her, found your blanket and doll in the hall. But the house started tumbling down. I knew I had to get out to keep you safe from *him*. So I had to leave her."

There was a moment of silence in the room, and then Ida shrugged. "But that's the past." She smiled bravely at Angie. "You're the future. You and the eye magnet."

Angie smiled through a veil of tears. "After Boone and I showed up at the cemetery, when did you figure out who I was?"

"You're the image of your mother, so I suspected when I was watching you argue with Boone the first day. But I couldn't believe it. Then Rick did a background check and found out your maiden name, and you said it was your sister Donaldson was engaged to, which tied you to him. I had to believe it. It made me more sure of his identity.

"I just didn't know what to do at first. I couldn't tell you who I was. Your father came to see me after I dropped you off and made me promise. It was for your own protection. Who knew if Donaldson could get to you through watching me?"

"We're together now," Angie said. "That's what counts."

"Yes. And as of right now, the past is officially over," Ida said. "We've got a new start. For some of us it will be wonderful." She beamed at both Angie and Boone. "And for others, it's going to be very difficult." She glanced at Madeleine, who was coming back in from the kitchen.

"Speaking of which, if you don't mind, I'm going to go upstairs and see if Chloe needs anything," Madeleine told them.

They all nodded solemnly.

"Since you're fine and dandy, I'm going to head on home." Ida got up with a groan and rubbed her knee. "I've got to stop all this detective stuff. It's too much on an old woman."

"You're not old," Angie protested. "It's late, though, and it's a long drive. Do you want to stay?"

Ida gave her a "perish the thought" look.

"You have your cell phone?"

Ida frowned, thinking. "It's in the other car."

"Then take mine, so I don't worry."

"Such fussing," Ida said. But she looked pleased. "You're gonna come visit me a lot, right?"

"Try and keep me away." Angie reached up and hugged her when Ida bent down, and gave her cheek a kiss.

"Too much love," Ida muttered, and waved, and then she was gone.

Leaning forward, Boone took her hand, too. "Do you want to talk now, or later, after you've had a chance to recuperate some?"

"Now." Angie wanted him to know everything and to understand what a difference he'd made in her life. "I'm so sorry I didn't talk to Madeleine a long time ago about my past. You were right to push me into doing it."

She briefly filled him in on her father's affair with her birth mother and all the aftermath. "I was a constant reminder of everything Madeleine had given up and the security of being loved by her husband that she'd lost. That's why she acted like she did. She apologized, and I forgave her."

"So you aren't worried about being a mother anymore?"

"Not at all." She grinned. "Of course we'll have to go through more negotiations first and hammer out the legal issues like marriage. Hmm. Maybe I'll need a lawyer."

"I come pro bono. No strings attached." His smile was wider than hers, but then his face grew serious. "Before we start, I have one more question. Madeleine told me you put down your weapon. Angel, why?"

"I had to show Donaldson I forgave him, and that I trusted he was a different person now that he believed in God than he was when he killed my mother."

"That's a huge trust you have in God," Boone said in wonder.

The edges of her lips turned up. "I *was* wearing the body armor, Boone."

He smiled back at her.

"I had to do it," she told him, more serious now. "I had to show him I believed in his efforts to know God and change his life. Plus it was his eyes. They changed. He was sorry, I know he was. All he wanted was to have a family, and I understand that."

Boone understood it, too. He squeezed her hand. "You're a really good person, Angie."

"Not so good. I'm still having problems forgiving Chief Gregg, even though he died." She shook her head. "But I'm going to pray about it."

"About those negotiations for marriage?"

The sadness left her eyes, and she met his, waiting.

"I'm sorry, too. I was wrong not to have trusted your instincts about Detry—Donaldson. I'm not ever making that mistake again.

When Ida called and told me you were going after Donaldson, I prayed the entire drive here. I was hoping God would open my eyes as to what He's about and help me see what I'm missing.

"Then I came through that door and saw you lying on the floor, shot, but found out you were going to be okay." He took a huge breath and let it out. "I knew that had to be God working— because it certainly hadn't been me who saved you. I cannot control everything, you were right about that, too. I have to trust in God again. And I'll never put you second to my work ever again. I promise you that."

Angie was filled with wonder. God had used her getting shot to get Boone to open his heart to Him. And to her. She couldn't have asked for more.

"Do you forgive me for doing that to you at the trial?" Boone asked.

"Of course."

Angie felt the warm, welcome pressure of his hands squeezing hers again and saw the love reflected in his eyes. He leaned forward and kissed her like she'd never been kissed before, a kiss of promise and of deep love that she knew, in her heart, God would bless. She kissed him back, her heart singing with happiness.

"I love you, Angie," Boone said.

"I love you, too."

Angie's heart soared. "Negotiations are over. Whenever you want to get married, I'm ready."

"Sounds good to me. Just name the date." He grinned and added, "See, I let you take control there."

She let go of his hand and poked him, and then she grabbed his neck and made him kiss her again. Just then, Boone's cell phone chirped out a song she hadn't heard on his cell before.

"I've got to get that," Boone said.

She slowly focused in on the tune as he answered.

"Yes, Ida, we're getting married… Yes, you did tell me so… I will…" Boone laughed, and hung up. "Ida said I should take care of you."

"You are." She let him kiss her one more time. *"Unforgettable?* That's what you programmed into your phone as my song? I like it."

"Good thing." He gave her a lopsided, boyish look. "Because that's one thing I'm not changing for you."

"I wouldn't have it any other way."

EPILOGUE

Two years later...

"Here she is," Angie said, handing baby Belinda to her sister, who had come to visit her and Boone at their lakeside home just outside of Copper City. "Just remember the deal you offered—if you don't tell me this secret you have, you have to give her back."

"Okay, okay," Chloe said, cuddling the infant in her arms and making kissing noises as Angie settled onto the sofa alongside Boone. "Jack's quitting the sheriff's department and starting a private detective agency."

Angie's eyes latched on to Boone's. Jack's divorce over a year before had been surprising enough. This was a real shocker.

"I guess that makes sense in a strange way," she told Boone. "You said he's been talking about changing his life. But I'm surprised he didn't tell you first."

"So am I," Boone said. Angie watched him regard her sister with a speculative look and turned one on Chloe herself. Her sister kept her head bowed as she played with Belinda. But she was smiling.

It took Angie a couple more seconds, but the smile finally gave Chloe away. "You're dating Jack and you never told us," she said. "You give me my baby back."

Chloe began giggling. "Actually, we're not dating anymore."

Angie stared at her. "No?"

"No, we're getting married tomorrow. That's why I'm here. I wanted to invite you and Boone."

"Tomorrow?" She cut a hard look at Boone, who was grinning. "You knew and didn't tell me."

"I did not," Boone insisted. "Besides, I wouldn't keep something like that from you. I'm afraid of you."

Angie slapped his arm.

Boone laughed harder. "I just think it's funny that your sister and my best friend were dating and neither of us figured it out."

"I don't. Tomorrow? Why didn't you tell us?" Angie asked her.

Chloe's lips twisted to keep from laughing and scaring the baby. "I waited till the last minute just in case you had any objections to this husband."

Angie groaned.

"Chloe," Boone said, "maybe you better delete the part of the vows about if anybody here knows any reason why this couple—"

"You two are really funny," Angie interrupted, trying to sound irritated, when she wasn't. Not at all. She beamed at Chloe. "Why didn't you bring Jack with you so we can congratulate him?"

"I did. He's waiting in the car for me to break the news. He's afraid of Angie, too."

Angie giggled. "All this fear could come in handy someday, you never know."

Boone headed outside to get him, and Angie perched on the edge of her seat, focused on her sister. "I'm so glad for you, Chloe. You two are perfect for each other."

Chloe nodded solemnly. "He actually asked me last year, after he became a Christian, but I put it off because he was thinking about quitting his job. You know how I am about money and security."

"Yeah." The same way she'd been about love. "But you worked it out?"

"I finally realized I had to give the financial part of my life to God, like I do everything else. We're going to put off having a baby for a couple of years until Jack's agency is established, and then we'll see what God holds in store for us."

They could hear the men in the hallway, and Chloe rose and handed Belinda back to Angie so she could hug her soon-to-be husband.

They stayed for a half hour, just long enough for Angie to see how much in love the two were. By the time she closed the door after them, Boone thought she was glowing as much as Chloe.

"I think they're perfect for each other," Angie said, leaning back against the door, closing her eyes dreamily, and sighing with happiness. The Lord had blessed her with all the love and family she could possibly want, and now he was blessing her sister, too. "God is a wonderful matchmaker."

"And you didn't have to do a thing."

"You made sense when you said hands-off, that I might be interfering with God's will if Jack's ex-wife came back." He'd been right. "See, I am listening to you."

"So what am I saying now?" He brushed her soft hair away from her cheek, leaned down and gave her a long, wonderful kiss.

"Boone?" she said when he pulled back. "I don't know what you're saying, but talk some more."

Picking her up in his arms, he did.

* * * * *

Dear Reader,

For the first three years after I became a Christian, I was faith-filled, but tentative. Was I praying right? Must I always forgive, even if people aren't sorry for what they did? If I told people about Jesus to help them, what should I say? And if I couldn't answer their difficult questions about God, would I turn them away from Him?

As a newer Christian faced with a deadly dilemma, Angie Delitano runs into all those questions in *DEADLY REUNION*. She must reunite with her former fiancé, who betrayed her, so he can be her bodyguard as she tries, alone, to save her estranged sister from a suspected wife-killer.

Boone Walker knows the woman he still loves is a Christian and watches her to see if a God he doesn't comprehend has really changed her life for the better. He needs something to fill the void he's felt since she broke their engagement. He thinks it's her. She thinks it's God.

I loved writing *DEADLY REUNION* for Steeple Hill and showing how faith in God and forgiveness can impact people's lives. I welcome reader letters at prowriter@excite.com or at www.shoutlife.com/FlorenceCase.

All the best,

Florence Case

QUESTIONS FOR DISCUSSION

1. Angie doesn't mention God to Ida at one point because she's afraid Ida will have hard questions for her that she doesn't know the answers to. Have you ever been worried about that? Should that stop us from witnessing? What is the solution?

2. Angie tries to consistently pray for God's guidance and for His will to be shown to her before she takes action. Do you do that? Are there other ways in addition to prayer for figuring out what God's will is for you?

3. If going to mature Christians for advice is mentioned when it comes to figuring out what God's will is for you, how do you know when their advice is godly and if you should follow it?

4. Do you seek God's help for every problem, no matter how small, or just for the big ones, as Angie does? Could there be a benefit in turning to God with tiny problems?

5. Before becoming a Christian, what Angie put first in her life (her passion) was finding love, because she believed it brought security. For a while, it did. If you can find security—and with it happiness—on your own, why do you believe you need God?

6. Boone's wanting to take total control of everything so nothing bad happens to him and those he loves is what makes him feel secure. Why is this unworkable when it comes to Angie?

7. What is Chloe's passion? How does she change by the end of the book?

8. Do you trust God for your security and happiness? Do you have any passion or goal that might be standing in the way of that?

9. Angie puts off returning to her mother's house. Why? Do you think she is purposely avoiding her past, or that she really just doesn't feel prepared to save her sister?

10. When Boone pushes Angie into going back to Newton, is he being selfish, or is he playing the role of protector by wanting her to be hidden and safe? Are there times when our motivations can be both selfish and good?

11. Boone has a hard time believing that God is really there. What happened when he was a child that made him think that? What could the members of his family's church at that time have done differently? What could his mother, as a believer, have done differently?

12. Angie runs into the need to forgive many times. Who does she end up forgiving, and why? Who does she not forgive, and why do you think that is? Do you agree with her for not forgiving in that case?

13. What does God say in the Bible about forgiveness? See Ephesians 4:32 and Luke 24:47. Does God require being sorry and repenting before He forgives? Why is it sometimes very difficult to forgive someone?

14. A popular saying is "I'll forgive, but I won't forget." Does that meet God's criteria for forgiveness?

15. What do you think you'll remember most about this story?

Turn the page for a sneak peek of RITA® Award-winner
Linda Goodnight's heartwarming story,
HOME TO CROSSROADS RANCH.
On sale in March 2009 from
Steeple Hill Love Inspired®.

Chapter One

Nate Del Rio heard screams the minute he stepped out of his Ford F-150 SuperCrew and started up the flower-lined sidewalk leading to Rainy Jernagen's house. He double-checked the address scribbled on the back of a bill for horse feed. Sure enough, this was the place.

Adjusting his Stetson against a gust of March wind, he rang the doorbell, expecting the noise to subside. It didn't.

Somewhere inside the modest, tidy-looking brick house, at least two kids were screaming their heads off in what sounded to his experienced ears like fits of temper. A television blasted out Saturday-morning cartoons.

He punched the doorbell again. Instead of the expected *ding-dong,* a raucous alternative Christian rock band added a few more decibels to the noise level.

Nate shifted the toolbox to his opposite hand and considered running for his life while he had the chance.

Too late. The bright red door whipped open. Nate's mouth fell open with it.

When the men's ministry coordinator from Bible Fellowship

had called him, he'd somehow gotten the impression that he was coming to help a little old schoolteacher. In his mind, that meant the kind who only drives to school and church and has a big, fat cat.

Not so. The woman standing before him with taffy-blond hair sprouting from a disheveled ponytail couldn't possibly be any older than his own thirty-one years. A big blotch of something purple stained the front of her white sweatshirt and she was bare-footed. Plus, she had a crying baby on each hip and a little red-haired girl hanging on one leg, bawling like a sick calf. And there wasn't a cat in sight.

What had he gotten himself into?

"May I help you?" she asked over the racket. Her blue-gray eyes were too unfocused and bewildered for his comfort.

Raising his voice, he asked, "Are you Ms. Jernagen?"

"Yes," she said cautiously. "I'm Rainy Jernagen. And you are…"

"Nate Del Rio."

She blinked, uncomprehending, all the while jiggling both babies up and down. One grabbed a hank of her hair. She flinched, her head angling to one side as she said, still cautiously, "Okaaay."

Nate reached out and untwined the baby's sticky fingers.

A relieved smile rewarded him. "Thanks. Is there something I can help you with?"

He hefted the red toolbox to chest level so she could see it. "From the Handy Man Ministry. Jack Martin called. Said you had a washer problem."

Understanding dawned. "Oh, my goodness. Yes. I'm so sorry. You aren't what I expected. Please forgive me."

She wasn't what he'd expected, either. Not in the least. Young and with a houseful of kids. He suppressed a shiver. Kids, even grown ones, could drive a person to distraction. He should know. His adult sister and brother were, at this moment, making his life as miserable as possible. The worst part was they did it all the time. Only this morning his sister, Janine, had finally packed up and gone back to Sal, giving Nate a few days' reprieve.

"Come in, come in," the woman was saying. "It's been a crazy morning, what with the babies showing up at 3:00 a.m. and Katie having a sick stomach. Then, while I was doing the laundry, the washing machine went crazy. Water everywhere." She jerked her chin toward the inside of the house. "You're truly a godsend."

He wasn't so sure about that, but he'd signed up for his church's ministry to help single women and the elderly with those pesky little handyman chores like oil changes and leaky faucets. Most of his visits had been to older ladies who plied him with sweet tea and jars of homemade jam and talked about the good old days while he replaced a fuse or unstopped the sink. And their houses had been quiet. Real quiet.

Rainy Jernagen stepped back, motioned him in, and Nate very cautiously entered a room that should have had flashing red lights and a Danger Zone sign.

Toys littered the living room like Christmas morning. An over-turned cereal bowl flowed milk onto a coffee table. Next to a playpen crowding one wall, a green package belched out dispos-able diapers. Similarly, baby clothes were strewn, along with a couple of kids' outfits on the couch and floor. In a word, the place was a wreck.

"The washer is back this way behind the kitchen. Watch your step. It's slippery."

More than slippery. Nate kicked his way through the living room and the kitchen area, though the kitchen actually appeared much tidier than the rest, other than the slow seepage of water coming from somewhere beyond. The shine of liquid glistening on beige tile led them straight to the utility room.

"I turned the faucets off behind the washer when this first started, but a tubful still managed to pump out onto the floor." She hoisted the babies higher on her hips and spoke to a young boy sitting on the floor. "Joshua, get out of those suds."

"But they're pretty, Miss Rainy." The brown-haired boy with bright blue eyes grinned up at her, extending a handful of bubbles. Light reflected off each droplet. "See the rainbows? There's always a rainbow, like you said. A rainbow behind the rain."

Rainy smiled at the child. "Yes, there is. But right now Mr. Del Rio needs to get in here to fix the washer. It's a little crowded for all of us." She was right about that. The space was no bigger than a small bathroom. "Can I get you to take the babies to the playpen while I show him around?"

"I'll take them, Miss Rainy." An older boy with a serious face and brown plastic glasses entered the room. Treading carefully, he came forward and took both babies, holding them against his slight chest. Another child appeared behind him. This one a girl with very blond hair and eyes the exact blue of Joshua's. How many children did this woman have, anyway? Six?

A heavy, smothery feeling pressed against his airway. Six kids?

Before he could dwell on that disturbing thought, a scream of massive proportions rent the soap-fragrant air. He whipped around, ready to protect and defend.

The little blond girl and the redhead were going at it.

"It's mine." Blondie tugged hard on a doll.

"It's mine. Will said so." To add emphasis to her demand, the redhead screamed bloody murder. "Miss Rainy!"

At about that time, Joshua decided to skate across the suds, and then slammed into the far wall next to a door that probably opened into the garage. He grabbed his big toe and set up a howl. Water sloshed as Rainy rushed forward and gathered him into her arms.

"Rainy!" Blondie screamed again.

"Rainy!" the redhead yelled.

Nate cast a glance at the garage exit and considered a fast escape.

Lord, I'm here to do a good thing. Can you help me out a little?

Rainy, her clothes now wet, somehow managed to take the doll from the fighting girls while snuggling Joshua against her side. The serious-looking boy stood in the doorway, a baby on each hip, taking in the chaos.

"Come on, Emma," the boy said to Blondie. "I'll make you some chocolate milk." So they went, slip-sliding out of the flooded room.

Four down, two to go.

Nate clunked his toolbox onto the washer and tried to ignore the chaos. Not an easy task, but one he'd learned to deal with as a boy. As an adult, he did everything possible to avoid this kind of madness. The Lord had a sense of humor sending him to this particular house.

"I apologize, Mr. Del Rio," Rainy said, shoving at the wads of hair that hung around her face like Spanish moss.

"Call me Nate. I'm not that much older than you." At thirty-one and the longtime patriarch of his family, he might feel seventy, but he wasn't.

"Okay, Nate. And I'm Rainy. Really, it's not usually this bad. I can't thank you enough for coming over. I tried to get a plumber, but it being Saturday…" She shrugged, letting the obvious go unsaid. No one could get a plumber on the weekend.

"No problem." He removed his white Stetson and placed it next to the toolbox. What was he supposed to say? That he loved wading through dirty soap suds and listening to kids scream and cry? Not likely.

Rainy stood with an arm around each of the remaining children—the rainbow boy and the redhead. Her look of embarrassment had him feeling sorry for her. All these kids and no man around to help. With this many, she'd never find another husband, he was sure of that. Who would willingly take on a boatload of kids?

After a minute, Rainy and the remaining pair left the room and he got to work. Wiggling the machine away from the wall wasn't easy. Even with all the water on the floor, a significant amount remained in the tub. This leftover liquid sloshed and gushed at regular intervals. In minutes, his boots were dark with moisture. No problem there. As a rancher, he often found his boots dark with lots of things, the best of which was water.

On his haunches, he surveyed the back of the machine, where hoses and cords and metal parts twined together like a nest of water moccasins.

As he investigated each hose in turn, he once more felt a presence in the room. Pivoting on his heels, he discovered the two boys squatting beside him, attention glued to the back of the washer.

"A busted hose?" the oldest one asked, pushing up his glasses.

"Most likely."

"I coulda fixed it, but Rainy wouldn't let me."

"That so?"

"Yeah. Maybe. If someone would show me."

Nate suppressed a smile. "What's your name?"

"Will. This here's my brother, Joshua." He yanked a thumb at the younger one. "He's nine. I'm eleven. You go to Miss Rainy's church?"

"I do, but it's a big church. I don't think we've met before."

"She's nice. Most of the time. She never hits us or anything, and we've been here for six months."

It occurred to Nate then that these were not Rainy's children. The kids called her "Miss Rainy," not "Mom," and according to Will they had not been here forever. But what was a young single woman doing with all these kids?

* * * * *

Look for
HOME TO CROSSROADS RANCH
by Linda Goodnight,
on sale March 2009
only from Steeple Hill Love Inspired®,
available wherever books are sold.

Love Inspired®

What do you do when Mr. Right doesn't want kids? Rainy Jernagen and her houseful of foster children won't let a little thing like that get in the way of bringing handyman Nate Del Rio home to them once and for all.

Look for

Home to Crossroads Ranch

by

Linda Goodnight

Available March wherever books are sold, including most bookstores, supermarkets, drugstores and discount stores.

Steeple
Hill®

LI87521

REQUEST YOUR FREE BOOKS!

2 FREE RIVETING INSPIRATIONAL NOVELS
PLUS 2 FREE MYSTERY GIFTS

YES! Please send me 2 FREE Love Inspired® Suspense novels and my 2 FREE mystery gifts (gifts are worth about $10). After receiving them, if I don't wish to receive any more books, I can return the shipping statement marked "cancel". If I don't cancel, I will receive 4 brand-new novels every month and be billed just $4.24 per book in the U.S. or $4.74 per book in Canada, plus 25¢ shipping and handling per book and applicable taxes, if any*. That's a savings of over 20% off the cover price! I understand that accepting the 2 free books and gifts places me under no obligation to buy anything. I can always return a shipment and cancel at any time. Even if I never buy another book, the two free books and gifts are mine to keep forever.

123 IDN ERXX 323 IDN ERXM

Name	(PLEASE PRINT)	
Address		Apt. #
City	State/Prov.	Zip/Postal Code

Signature (if under 18, a parent or guardian must sign)

Order online at www.LoveInspiredSuspense.com
Or mail to Steeple Hill Reader Service:

IN U.S.A.: P.O. Box 1867, Buffalo, NY 14240-1867
IN CANADA: P.O. Box 609, Fort Erie, Ontario L2A 5X3

Not valid to current subscribers of Love Inspired Suspense books.

Want to try two free books from another series?
Call 1-800-873-8635 or visit www.morefreebooks.com

* Terms and prices subject to change without notice. N.Y. residents add applicable sales tax. Canadian residents will be charged applicable provincial taxes and GST. Offer not valid in Quebec. This offer is limited to one order per household. All orders subject to approval. Credit or debit balances in a customer's account(s) may be offset by any other outstanding balance owed by or to the customer. Please allow 4 to 6 weeks for delivery. Offer available while quantities last.

Your Privacy: Steeple Hill Books is committed to protecting your privacy. Our Privacy Policy is available online at www.SteepleHill.com or upon request from the Reader Service. From time to time we make our lists of customers available to reputable third parties who may have a product or service of interest to you. If you would prefer we not share your name and address, please check here. ☐

Love Inspired SUSPENSE

TITLES AVAILABLE NEXT MONTH

Available March 10, 2009

POISONED SECRETS by Margaret Daley
An anonymous tip brought Maggie Ridgeway to her birth mother. Yet finding her led to more questions. Why did her parents abandon her? What's triggering the *multiple* burglaries in her new apartment? Can building owner Kane McDowell protect her? And once he finds out who she really is, will he still want to?

COLD CASE MURDER by Shirlee McCoy
Without a Trace
Loomis, Louisiana, holds no charms for Jodie Gilmore. Still, the novice FBI agent has a job to do, investigating the local missing person's case. But the job gets complicated when handsome forensic anthropologist Harrison Cahill uncovers a decades-old double homicide.

A SILENT TERROR by Lynette Eason
There was no motive for the murder—Marianna Santino's roommate shouldn't have died. Then Detective Ethan O'Hara realizes the deaf teacher was the *real* target. Ethan learns all he can about Marianna. Soon, he's willing to risk everything—even his heart—to keep her safe.

PERFECT TARGET by Stephanie Newton
The corpse in her path was the first warning. Next was a break-in at Bayley Foster's home. She's certain that the stalker who once tormented her has returned to toy with her again. Her protective neighbor, police detective Cruse Conyers, is determined to get answers—at any cost.

LISCNMBPA0209